THE REAL
SILENT
WITNESSES

THE REAL
SILENT
WITNESSES

SHOCKING CASES FROM THE
WORLD OF FORENSIC SCIENCE

WENSLEY CLARKSON

WELBECK

Published by Welbeck
An imprint of Welbeck Non-Fiction Limited,
part of Welbeck Publishing Group.
20 Mortimer Street,
London W1T 3JW

First published by Welbeck in 2021

A CIP catalogue record for this book is available from the British Library

ISBN
Paperback - 9781787395619
eBook - 9781787395626

Typeset by seagulls.net
Printed and bound in the UK

10 9 8 7 6 5 4 3 2 1

www.welbeckpublishing.com

CONTENTS

FOREWORD

By Nigel McCrery, creator of *Silent Witness*

As a writer, I am probably better known for my works of fiction, like the BBC series *Silent Witness* and *New Tricks*. However, before becoming a writer I served as a police officer in Nottinghamshire, dealing with crimes of every nature, from murder to burglary. As this book rightly points out, it is from many of these true-life crimes and the people I encountered while dealing with them that I drew inspiration for many of my fictional characters and stories.

Probably the best known of these is the Home Office pathologist Professor Helen Whitwell. Helen is without doubt one of the brightest people I have ever met, writing several books on her subject, including *Mason's Forensic Medicine for Lawyers*. During her long and illustrious career, Helen worked for both the prosecution and the defence and became one of the world's leading experts on Shaken Baby Syndrome. Yet despite her outstanding academic qualifications, she is certainly not like the nerdy boffins normally associated with the job. An elegant woman in every respect, she enjoys champagne breakfasts, fine dining and high-quality wines and spirits. Yet there is a slightly eccentric side to Helen which made her interesting and the perfect character for any work of forensic fiction; I certainly could never have made Helen up. She would get lost en route to murder scenes and, before the age of the infamous mobile phone, would call the control room, give them the number she was calling from, and the investigating officers would have to send a car and a detective to find her and bring her to the location. On another occasion, during the early hours of the morning, she arrived at the murder scene after the press and TV cameras. Reversing up an unknown person's drive, she opened her bag, which I thought would be full of the tools of her trade: a scalpel and bottles of various sizes and uses. Instead of producing those, she produced a make-up bag, hairbrush and perfume, announcing that if we thought she was going to face the press at 3 a.m. without her "slap" on, we could think again. When she had examined herself thoroughly, we moved on to the scene. Probably my favourite characteristic, however, was her heavily scented garden, each plant and flower selected for its particular aroma. I hadn't realized she was such a keen gardener and told her so. To my surprise, she replied that she wasn't: in fact, she didn't really enjoy gardening. So, I pointed out, why the beautiful garden? Her reply was both interesting and surprising. Pathologists are famous for losing their sense of smell. It's not the pungent and often putrefying smell of the bodies but the chemicals used during the examinations that can damage your senses. As soon as she could no longer smell her garden, or the strong aromas dimmed, she would retire. Some years later, she did.

New Tricks was once again based partially on characters I had met, and often worked with, during my service. Many of the more bizarre incidents and storylines were also based on things I had witnessed or been involved with. As a reader as well as a writer of crime fiction, it became clear very quickly that, as is well illustrated in this book, fiction only illustrates and at times illuminates crime, but nothing comes close to truly representing it, as human emotions and the motives of the individual, however odd and unfathomable, drive an investigation forward.

As suspects become more aware of their rights within the law, the job of the detective has become increasingly difficult. Many, especially professional criminals, will refuse to say a word, relying on phrases such as "no comment" – the standard reply recommended by defence solicitors. Eyewitness evidence is also often, under cross-examination, being brought into question and uncertainty. As a result of this, forensic science plays an ever more significant role in delivering important evidence to the attention of a jury or magistrate – of a kind that is increasingly difficult to refute or challenge.

Using forensic science within a criminal investigation is basically about identification. Forensic investigation is concerned primarily with piecing together the disparate clues left at a scene in order to form a coherent picture of events and, crucially, to establish the identities of those involved – or, equally importantly, those who were not. The anthropologist Margaret Mead (1901–78) said, "Always remember that you are absolutely unique. Just like everybody else". It is within this uniqueness of the individual that forensic science is based and thrives. Alphonse Bertillon (1853–1914), the French scientist and criminologist, pioneered not only the use of photographs and a basic method of photo-fit but also established a method of identification based on a person's unique measurements: length of nose, fingers, arms, feet, et cetera. He calculated that if eleven measurements on an individual matched eleven on the suspect, the chances of them not being the guilty person was four million to one. After initial struggles within a doubting scientific community, he was hailed as the greatest criminologist of his day. However, following his failure to trace the criminal who had stolen the Mona Lisa, despite a large palm print being found on the glass that had covered the painting, his methods, while not entirely dismissed, were largely discredited. From then on, the science of fingerprinting started to gather traction.

Today we live in the age of DNA, a process of identification which was honed by the scientists Sir Alex Jeffrey and Peter Gill while researching at Leicester University. This method was first used to solve the Narborough Murders, when it led not only to the discovery of Colin Pitchfork, the killer of two teenage girls, Lynda Mann and Dawn Ashworth, but to the exoneration of the police's main suspect, who was subsequently released. DNA has now been used to solve thousands of crimes, both recent and historic, as it continues to be refined.

Writers of fiction will continue to use forensic science as a method of leading their fascinated readers towards their hidden culprit. They seldom have to cope with the everyday realities of a complicated and often drawn-out enquiry. Real investigators, as illustrated in this book, do not have the privileges of fiction. They have to work within legal limits, budgets and what, in reality, forensic science is genuinely capable of. In fiction, cost fails to be an issue, and if the science doesn't quite work, well, you can always stretch a point. In many ways, true crime illustrates far better the work of an investigating team and their interaction with forensic science. It's this interaction that makes *The Real Silent Witnesses* one of the most fascinating books on the subject.

My patients never complain.
If their illness is perplexing,
I can always put them back
in the refrigerator.

KEITH SIMPSON,
LEGENDARY BRITISH FORENSIC SCIENTIST.

SILENT WITNESS
A LEGAL DEFINITION

A theory or rule in the law of evidence that is produced by a process whose reliability is established and may be admitted as substantive evidence of what it depicts, without the need for an eyewitness to verify the accuracy of its depiction.

AUTHOR'S NOTE

The heroes and heroines of this book are without doubt the forensic scientists. So to any whom I have failed to mention here, I humbly apologize. Your skills have not gone unnoticed. I simply don't have enough room in this book to highlight all your successes!

Most of us find it hard to talk about death, especially if it concerns someone close to us. But when it's compressed into a dramatic TV series, we seem content to lap it up. I've tried to gauge the levels of taste required when writing a book like this, but apologies to anyone who feels I've strayed into overly graphic territory with some of the material you are about to read.

Many of the experts I spoke to for this book preferred not to be named because they want their work to do the "talking". They felt that the general public might presume they were in some way "cashing in" on the misery of others.

So to protect the heroes (as well as the criminals), some of the names and details of certain individuals featured here have been changed. The aim is to protect people's privacy while at the same time maintaining the integrity of all the stories featured here.

DEDICATION

To The Three Musketeers.
They came. They saw. They conquered.

Three legendary forensic scientists dealt with virtually all
the suspicious deaths in the London area across much of
the twentieth century. They even jointly sifted remains from
serial killer policeman John Christie's sordid murders at 10
Rillington Place, Notting Hill. They often dined together,
when they'd discuss all their most chilling cases. As a result,
they became known as "The Three Musketeers":

Professor Francis Camps (1905–72) carried out an
astonishing 90,000 post-mortems and was renowned for
smoking at the post-mortem table, often dribbling ash onto
a corpse. He was once called in by the Museum of London to
examine the undershirt said to have been worn by Charles I
to his execution.

Professor Keith Simpson (1907–85) came to prom-
inence in London during the Second World War, when he
carried out autopsies on more than a hundred victims crushed

in a stampede at Bethnal Green Underground station. In 1942, he examined a body found in a bombed church and deduced it was a woman murdered by her husband and hidden in the rubble. Simpson also examined the corpse of Lord Lucan's murdered nanny.

Professor Donald Teare (1911–79) worked on the notorious "cleft chin murder" case, in which a rogue London taxi driver was shot for a trivial sum of money by a US army deserter during World War Two. Teare helped solve numerous other murder mysteries but liked to keep out of the limelight, even more than his two colleagues.

INTRODUCTION

My first encounter with anyone inside the world of forensic science came in a rundown, smokey pub in south London, in the late 1970s. I was a rookie crime reporter on the local newspaper and part of my job was to share a drink or two with the local CID (plain clothes) officers from the nearby police station.

On one rainy April night in 1978, the chief of detectives introduced me to a scruffy, nicotine-encrusted man in his mid-thirties who turned out to be Dr Iain West, already well on his way to becoming one of the UK's most renowned forensic scientists. At that time, he was resident Forensic Pathologist at Guy's and St Thomas' hospitals, in London. West prided himself on coming up with the unexpected – and he made it clear in the pub that night that he wasn't afraid to express his opinion on subjects that extended way beyond legal and scientific boundaries.

When giving evidence in court, West's testimony had always made him appear to be a grave, intense, somewhat aloof personality who was sometimes even at loggerheads with the police he was often supposed to be working alongside. The pervasive whiff of mortuary disinfectant followed Iain West wherever he went. He liked this because it told people who he was without his even having to introduce himself.

Iain West had first been inspired to take up forensic pathology during his time at Addenbrooke's Hospital, Cambridge, under highly respected forensic scientist Professor Austin Gresham, whose enthusiasm soon rubbed off on the young medic. In 1974, West moved to the forensic department at St Thomas' hospital, London. Four years later he took up a post in the forensic medicine department at London's Guy's and St Thomas' hospitals, led by the legendary Professor Keith Simpson's protégé Professor Keith Mant. West took over from Mant in 1984 and remained at Guy's for the rest of his career. West's second wife Vesna Djurovic was another leading pathologist and member of the same Guy's department.

Iain West liked to pride himself on always being primarily concerned about the *now*. He was never wrapped up in research. He tended to leave that to others. But when it came to the actual cases, he was always focused, methodical, realistic and imaginative. In murder investigations, he prided himself on putting himself into the mind of the killer and working backwards from there to try and establish exactly what had happened at the scene of a crime. But despite West's claims to the contrary, he did actually think beyond "the now". At Guy's Hospital, he helped set up a computerized database filled with information and images relating to specific forensic cases. These files have since become vital reference sources for lawyers, police forces and pathologists across the globe and are reckoned to have helped solve numerous crimes.

The Iain West I met in that south London pub was about as far removed from being a typical scientist as you could get. Here was a loud, jokey party animal who couldn't wait to order some whiskies from the bar to chase down with the beers. On this particular evening, West clutched a pint of bitter in one hand and a cigarette in the other, and we got talking about rugby. In fact, he was more interested in swapping tales about his favourite sport than telling me about the UK murder mysteries he'd helped solve through his forensic skills.

We never specifically discussed any of Iain West's actual cases that night, but that was typical of his unique modus operandi. He used his surprisingly outgoing character to disarm me, and that in turn enabled him to avoid saying anything that he might later regret. He did tell me, though, that he was a keen rifleman with intimate knowledge of all types of firearms. He recalled with great relish how he liked to hunt wild boar in mainland Europe and boasted in a charming and self-effacing way about his marksmanship.

In 1984 – a few years after that meeting – police constable Yvonne Fletcher was shot dead by a sniper's bullet outside the Libyan Embassy in central London. West established through intricate forensic tests that the shot had been fired from within the building, which clearly implied she'd been deliberately targeted.

West also examined many of the bodies from several terrorist bombings, including 1982's Hyde Park attack and the bombing of Harrods in 1983. The following year he was called in to examine the victims of the IRA bombing of the

3

Grand Hotel, Brighton, which narrowly failed to kill Margaret Thatcher during that year's Conservative Party Conference.

Iain West's report on the 1988 Clapham rail disaster led to drastic modification of train carriages to help improve passenger safety. Eleven years later he was once again on his hands and knees at a rail disaster, sifting through the wreckage in Paddington.

West also carried out a post mortem on BBC TV presenter Jill Dando, who was killed in 1999 by a hitman on the doorstep of her home in Fulham, south-west London. West's forensic skills even played a part in the release of British Army soldier Lee Clegg, who'd been convicted of a murder when he was serving in Northern Ireland.

He told me that he dealt with all the psychological and emotionally draining aspects of his job by always keeping his thoughts to himself when he was out in the field. This "coolness under fire", combined with an almost photographic memory, meant that he was often able to flash back to his past case experiences with the flick of an eyelid and use that knowledge to help him move forward on a new case.

Dr West admitted to many journalists, including myself, that his own coping mechanism was to concentrate on the mechanics of every forensic assignment. That meant first of all dissecting the body, then measuring wounds and injuries. Dr West called this his "noting and observation stage". That's when his medical training would take over, and that further enabled him to mentally and emotionally block out the horror he so often witnessed first hand. But despite this, Iain West

4

suffered nightmares about the images he faced every day of his professional life. He once admitted: "I usually suffer from disturbed sleep for a few weeks after any of those type of mass death cases. I anticipate that as a normal human reaction. I find it goes away of its own accord."

Many who knew Iain West believe his eccentricity was at odds with the sombreness of his profession, as portrayed by many TV adaptations, including *Silent Witness*. He really was a one-off. From a personal perspective, my unlikely meeting with Iain West in that south London pub taught me one thing: that all of us, however clever and insightful, need a release from our intense work environment in order to move on further in the world and achieve our own personal goals in life. And the thing I remember most about that drunken night took place at the very end. Just before he went home, West leaned over to me, very drunk but deadly serious, and said: "The truth is always more surprising than the lies. You have to have an absolute determination to tell the truth no matter how much pressure is put on you to come to a certain conclusion."

THE *SILENT WITNESS* EFFECT

There is no getting away from the fact that many of us have a morbid interest in death and crime. We can't help it. Most of it is down to the fact that television provides law-abiding citizens with a window into another world where all the usual moral lines are blurred. We can lose ourselves in a drama like *Silent Witness* for a few hours knowing full well that back in the real world our own safety zones are still in place.

My hope is that this book will be different from dozens of others that have delved into the mysteries of forensic science, in trying to present the facts in a way everyone can relate to.

Millions of people are out there glued to their screens every time a new episode of *Silent Witness* is televised. That in itself shows the depth of interest in this subject. In recent years, *Silent Witness* has increasingly concentrated on the more technical sides of pathology, while at the same time continuing to build a believable dramatic thread around every storyline. Obviously, this works, otherwise *Silent Witness* would have disappeared from our screens many years ago. But it is a credit to the show's creator and writers that it has managed to move with the times, as forensic science has taken great strides over the almost 30 years since the series first aired.

Silent Witness carefully constructs and highlights the science, and that's what makes it so different from most other murder shows. Everything is filmed from a forensic point of view, rather than that of the long arm of the law, or even of the criminals who've committed the crime in the first place.

This book aims to take a similar approach, as my intention all along has been to dig deep beneath the surface of often notorious crimes and reveal, for the first time, how forensics helped bring the guilty to justice but also ensured that the innocent avoided jail and, in some cases, the death penalty.

Rest assured, this book doesn't intend to gloss over the failures, either. They're just as important as the notable successes when it comes to understanding the story of forensic science's role in law enforcement, particularly in the United Kingdom and the United States of America. It's crucial not to omit forensic science's mistakes and the way that some of its findings can be twisted and misrepresented to suit the agenda of others.

Ultimately, this book hopes to inform and entertain readers by revealing the major forensic breakthroughs that have so often been ignored.

You don't have to be an avid fan of *Silent Witness* to read this book, either. It contains many intriguing characters and controversial real cases for anyone with a general interest in true crime.

I've attempted to make the action rise above the technical side of forensic science. I know some legitimate forensic experts will find that frustrating, but this book is for everyone. It's not intended as a reference book and the cases described here have as many dramatic twists and turns as any TV drama.

Most of these cases are in the public domain but I fully appreciate the *Silent Witness* team would have to alter and adjust them so they were not recognizable by the time they got onto the small screen. On TV, all blatant similarities to real and living persons must be removed in case the real people recognize themselves and seek legal recourse.

* * *

Sometimes, *Silent Witness* gives its viewers the impression – albeit unintentionally – that the most brilliant forensic minds come only from the UK. Nothing could be further from the truth. I have reported on crimes across the world and met many forensic scientists in other countries, from Australia to the United States to South America to Europe.

In Santiago, Chile, I tracked down a pathologist who performed an autopsy on an alleged British spy found dead in a hotel cupboard. He worked out of a rundown, underfunded laboratory in the roughest part of the city but showed immense bravery in allowing me to read his report, despite a government cover-up on the case.

While living in California in the early 1990s, I discovered that forensic science was taken so seriously that police investigators wouldn't attend a murder scene without a medical examiner being present. In most other Western world countries at that time, forensic experts still took second place to detectives when it came to on-site investigations.

* * *

Today – thanks in part to TV's *Silent Witness* – most of us fully appreciate what these forensic scientists do for society. Some even believe that their skills are tantamount to artistry. They have the patience of a painter or a writer as they analyze every possibility in their minds, until they can be sure of what everything means when it comes to the victim *and* the perpetrator of a crime.

The key to solving murders often lies with the personalities of these forensic scientists. They are analytical characters who have to chip away to uncover evidence. They don't seek out motives for crimes like the police do. They form their opinions around what they find. That means they look at things from a different perspective – and that helps them to solve the unsolvable.

These unique characters can ignore the pressures that their police associates face. They refuse to be rushed during their investigations, because accuracy – not speed – is their main objective. One former Scotland Yard murder squad detective explained: "I've seen other police officers constantly pressurize forensic scientists to provide fast feedback for their investigations. It's a very short-sighted attitude, which no doubt leads to some very questionable decisions. Police officers need to encourage a much friendlier atmosphere between us and them. We need safe and accurate results rather than the type of half guesses which used to happen in the bad old days of law enforcement."

Technical advances in communications mean that today everyone's movements can be tracked. Every phone call made can be traced. Every journey can be monitored. Every purchase is recorded. But none of that mountain of personal information means anything if there are no experts to analyze it, sift through it and connect it until they find what they're looking for.

PROLOGUE

A thin plume of grey smoke and the crackling sound of a bonfire were the only signs of activity in the grounds of the large, isolated detached house on the corner of dense woodland bordering a 500-acre country park in Essex. It was the middle of the summer of 2015. CCTV security cameras lined the driveway, recording every moment, 24 hours a day. And half a dozen bland, red "do not enter" signs could be seen through the late afternoon drizzle nailed to trees on the perimeter of the same property. From inside the house, the muffled sound of two Rottweilers barking furiously could be heard in the distance. They stood on hind legs pawing at the steamed-up double glass doors at the back of the house.

Just then, a young man and woman in their early twenties appeared inside the house and tried to calm the dogs down. Eventually, they dragged them into the sitting room and returned to open the double doors to the garden. Hesitantly, the couple crept out onto the patio shouting "Dad". When there was no reply, the young man turned towards the bonfire, still crackling noisily in the distance. Behind him, his girlfriend stopped as she saw something, arching her neck to get a better look. Grabbing her boyfriend by the arm, she pulled him around and pointed.

The young man froze momentarily in his tracks before rushing towards the crumpled body of his 64-year-old father; lifeless and contorted, it lay spread across the ground, his torso soaked in blood.

The son straddled the body and started trying to give him CPR, frantically thumping his chest. The young man later said he could feel the life draining out of his father. With the body limp beneath him, he stopped and struggled back onto his feet. Breathing heavily, he rang 999 on his mobile.

Within half an hour, paramedics arrived and were examining the corpse. They immediately noticed very recent "pre-existing wounds" to the body following major surgery and ruled out foul play. The victim had clearly died from natural causes after falling from his quad bike, slewed on the ground nearby.

"Are you sure it's his heart?" asked a young trainee paramedic, accompanying two senior colleagues who'd examined the corpse.

"Yeah, it's his heart. I've seen dozens like this one before," one of them said.

Two young police constables then arrived at the scene. They didn't even bother examining the corpse after being told that the man's wounds from recent gallbladder surgery had split open when he fell, which had caused him to bleed out. There was no point in even calling an inspector to the scene to confirm their assessment or checking the man's antecedents on the police national computer. It was, as they say, an open-and-shut case.

If those two police officers had bothered to make the normal checks, they would have discovered that the UK's National Crime Agency and Spanish police had had the victim under surveillance for the best part of 20 years.

Police ordered an autopsy as a matter of course because the death would be recorded as sudden, even though there were no suspicious circumstances. Less than an hour later, the corpse was gingerly loaded onto a gurney and taken away in a dark van with blacked-out windows to be stored in a morgue to await an examination by the next available pathologist.

It was an oddly muted end for a man feared and loathed throughout the underworld. Most had expected him to die in a hail of bullets after one feud too many. But instead, he'd keeled over in the middle of the grounds of his big house just like Marlon Brando's Don Corleone in *The Godfather*.

The body was kept in a deep freeze drawer at the Leicester University forensic pathology unit so that an expert could confirm what everyone already knew: that he'd died from what appeared to be a congenital heart defect and the after-effects of gallbladder surgery.

That corpse would remain refrigerated until highly respected forensic scientist Dr Benjamin Swift returned from a few days, leave to examine it, as he was obliged to do because of the sudden nature of the man's death. The victim's family were warned this might take four or five days, so they should not make any funeral arrangements for the time being, just to be on the safe side.

Five days later, pathologist Dr Swift returned from his early summer break. Less than two minutes after pulling open the drawer to the refrigeration unit containing the corpse, the medical examiner put down his instruments, walked to the phone attached to the wall in the corner of his laboratory, punched out a number and waited for a response.

"I think you'd better get over here as quickly as possible," he said.

That corpse had given up the secrets that everyone close to the victim had suspected all along. Dr Swift's post-mortem examination immediately found the man had been shot six times in the back, chest and arms. The gunmen had used special bullets that left minimal impact marks. When the news went public there was hell to pay.

Essex Police chiefs were hauled into Scotland Yard to explain themselves. This victim's name was so synonymous with police corruption that there were suspicions the police might have deliberately misdiagnosed the cause of death in order to give his killer more time to escape. When it became clear this was not the case and that Essex Police had quite simply been inefficient, the force's serious crime squad was given a no-holds-barred brief to immediately launch a major murder investigation.

Essex Police publicly admitted the man's death now "bore all the hallmarks of a professional hit". A contract killer had climbed over a fence into the garden and shot his victim at close range.

It was already a classic case of too little too late. The killer was long gone, and if it hadn't been for the skills of Dr Swift, no one would have even known that the gangland crime boss had been murdered. "Without the pathologist's examination, we might never have realized that criminal had been killed by a hitman in his own garden," one of the detectives involved in the case later told me. "Sometimes we don't give the scientists enough credit. It's not always about being clever and digging up the truth. Sometimes the truth is staring you in the face."

That in itself perfectly highlights the across-the-board importance of forensic scientists today. But in addition to this, there is another secret angle to this murder case, which links it directly to the popular television series *Silent Witness*, that has never before been publicly revealed. Pathologist Dr Benjamin Swift worked for many years as a consultant for the show. The production team behind *Silent Witness* could rightly point to these sort of professional "overlaps" as further proof that their immensely popular TV series more closely mirrors the real world than any other drama show in television history.

Most importantly, if the bullet-riddled corpse of that criminal had not been properly examined by a forensic expert, then a notorious gangland murder would have occurred without anyone ever being the wiser. "Yes, it was an open and shut case," added the same detective involved in this murder enquiry. "But that's not the point. We, the police, need to appreciate and listen to the experts, even when we think we have all the answers."

At a time when the UK government has already implemented cost cutting throughout the forensic science world, this is a chilling reminder of how people could get away with murder if forensic scientists were not used for each and every unexplained death. The police who attended the scene of that killing had assured their superior officers the victim had died of natural causes. Until 30 years ago, that would usually have meant *no* autopsy. As one forensic scientist explained to me recently: "If we went back to those dark days again because of cost cuts by the politicians, we might as well give criminals a gun and tell them to shoot all their enemies dead because often they'll no doubt get away with it."

* * *

In order to understand how forensic science evolved in the first place, one has to delve into the past, present and future of this most inexact of all sciences. That means revealing the characters that have had a big influence on the forensic world.

These forensic experts are a remarkable bunch. They first started to emerge on the criminal horizon more than two hundred years ago on London's mean and filthy slum-riddled streets. Those early pioneers were the scientific renegades of their times, in a sense. They broke the rules much more than Nicky or Tom in *Silent Witness*. But they did all that to further society's need to bring murderers and other criminals to justice.

In order to appreciate the *full* story of forensic science, one has to go much further back in time.

BEFORE *SILENT WITNESS*: THE HISTORY, THE SCIENCE AND THE SPECIALISTS

Everything and everyone that enters a crime scene leaves some piece of evidence behind. It is the key to all forensic investigations of crime scenes.

PROFESSOR EDMOND LOCARD, 1910

BACK IN TIME

The word "forensic" originated from the Latin word "*forensis*", which stands for a forum. The idea was that a forum of experts would examine subjects, collect evidence and jointly form a concrete opinion. The earliest known use of forensic science dates back to the ancient Greek and Roman societies, who made significant contributions to the field of medicine, in particular pharmacology. They uncovered and studied the production, use and symptoms of toxins, which went on to be particularly helpful when it came to studying past murder cases.

Today, scientists believe that the first-ever "autopsy" was performed in 3,000 BCE in the Egyptian civilization that ruled the world back then. But that only happened because it was a prerequisite for their religion to remove and examine internal organs after death.

In 44 BCE came the first "official" recorded autopsy, when a Roman physician called Antistius dissected the body of Roman politician and general Julius Caesar. That examination revealed that despite his having been stabbed twenty-three times, Caesar's death was caused by one knife wound through his chest. Antistius came to his ground-breaking conclusions after testing a selection of blades on animal carcasses and eventually matching one of the wounds to the one in Caesar's corpse. This showed that a specific type of dagger was the actual murder weapon.

Antistius got every participant in the stabbing of Caesar to hand in their knives to him. Legend has it that the killer eventually (and proudly) confessed when the smell of blood attracted swarms of flies to his weapon as he gave it to Antistius. No one was ever prosecuted for the murder of Caesar because those very same assailants took over the Roman Empire.

Centuries later came the earliest version of a polygraph test in ancient India. This involved the examination of the saliva, mouth and tongue of a suspect. After the suspect's mouth was filled with some dry rice, they were asked to spit it out. If the rice got stuck in their mouths, they were found guilty.

Four hundred years ago, the first reported autopsy in North America was performed by French colonists desperate to determine what was killing them as they endured a rugged winter on St. Croix island near what is now Portland, Maine. Nearly half of the 79 settlers led by explorers Pierre Dugua and Samuel de Champlain had died over that winter from malnutrition and the harsh weather. All this was uncovered when the skull of one man was found during excavations by the National Park Service just fifteen years ago. The top of the skull had been removed to expose the brain. It had been put back in place before the body was buried. It was the exact same procedure that forensic pathologists use during autopsies to this day.

Less than two centuries ago, crime scene investigators in London would taste the body fluids they found at a crime scene because it was the only way to identify what they were. Those supposedly upholding law and order at that time saw murders in strictly black and white terms. There was a body, which was usually followed by a confession or another body. If there were no bodies, solving these types of crimes was a mission impossible.

London back in those days was rife with crime and violence, and the continual inability of the police to solve heinous crimes left the upper classes horrified. They wanted to crack down on the criminals, so they started to fund the study of forensic sciences. As a result, a big breakthrough for forensics came shortly after that, when a fingerprint analysis system was developed by Sir Edward Henry – the commissioner of the Metropolitan Police of London. He established that the direction, flow, pattern and other characteristics of fingerprints gave them unique identifiable characteristics, and this established fingerprint analysis. Today the Henry Classification System remains the standard for criminal fingerprint analysis techniques across the globe.

In the eighteenth and nineteenth centuries there were other big forensic breakthroughs that combined the use of basic logic and science. The first occurred after the arrest of a man called John Toms in Lancaster for the murder of Edward Culshaw with a pistol. The wadding left by the murder weapon perfectly matched that of a weapon owned by Toms. There was also a torn piece of newspaper in Toms' pocket that matched a page that the victim had been reading. Encouraged by this discovery, one of Scotland Yard's most "pioneering" officers, Henry Goddard – who eventually became commissioner – established that it was possible to match a bullet to a murder weapon under detailed examination.

Other aspects of forensics began to bear fruit, thanks to the rich citizens of London funding these scientific investigators. In 1816, a farm labourer called Warwick was convicted of murder after police forensics collected and analyzed footprints and cloth impressions left on the damp soil of the crime scene near a pool where a young maid had been drowned. Those impressions matched boots and clothes belonging to Warwick and proved he was the killer of the maid.

It wasn't until 1836 that an Act of Parliament officially authorized payments towards forensic experts and the cost of post-mortems. In that same year a forensic scientist called James Marsh – based at the Royal Military Academy in Woolwich, south London, close to the River Thames – invented a reliable test for that most deadly of poisons – arsenic.

Marsh had been infuriated when he'd earlier been called as a chemist by the prosecution in the murder trial of a man who was accused of poisoning his grandfather with arsenic-laced coffee. Marsh had performed a standard test by mixing a suspected sample with hydrogen sulphide and hydrochloric acid, but by the time he showed the results to the jury, the sample had deteriorated and the suspect was acquitted on the basis of reasonable doubt. So Marsh developed a much better test by combining a sample containing arsenic with sulphuric acid and arsenic-free zinc, resulting in arsine gas. The gas was ignited, and it decomposed to pure metallic arsenic which, when passed to a cold surface, would appear as a silvery-black deposit. Marsh's cleverly devised test was so sensitive that it could detect as little as one-fiftieth of a milligram of arsenic.

In 1845, a man called John Tawell fled to London after the death of a former lover. It was only after detailed examination of the body that traces of cyanide were discovered and a murder hunt was launched. Tawell eventually became the first criminal arrested through the use of an electric telegraph. But even more importantly, an expert forensic witness was called for the first time at a criminal trial, and his evidence that the body contained traces of cyanide ensured Tawell was found guilty.

But these developments in forensics were relatively few and far between back then. For many subsequent years, a combination of restricted scientific data and sloppy detective work continued to make forensic medicine the most neglected side of worldwide law enforcement.

Forensic scientists were often treated as the opposition by police officers, who accused them of spending too long reaching their conclusions while the police remained under intense pressure to arrest anyone they could lay their hands on. As a result, these two crucial investigative forces were often frozen in a classic stand-off, and the cause of truth and justice suffered untold damage.

At the start of the twentieth century, interest in forensic science suddenly took off. New techniques began to be developed, mainly in laboratories in Britain, Europe and the United States. For the first time, law enforcement agencies started to appreciate how important forensic examinations could be when it came to murder.

In France in 1910, Professor Edmond Locard opened the world's first-ever fully equipped crime laboratory. His favourite phrase was "everything leaves a trace". This was to become what's now known as Locard's Exchange Principle, which was based on the idea that evidence was *always* present at the scene of a murder, whatever the circumstances. Locard also believed that everyone and everything takes some piece of the crime scene with them when they leave.

By the 1920s, bullet analysis had improved enormously thanks to the use of a powerful microscope, which further helped connect the relationship between bullets and the shell casing from which they were fired.

But despite all these developments in forensic science, crime continued to thrive. Soldiers with post-traumatic stress from the First World War were arriving back in UK cities penniless and suffering mental health problems. This, combined with a worldwide recession, saw many of them join criminal gangs throughout the country. As a result, the following two decades were probably the most murderous years in the history of the UK's twentieth-century crimelands. Many forensic scientists honed their skills during this period of time. But there was little else to celebrate in those interwar years.

In 1940, London was being carpeted with bombs dropped by the Germans during the early stages of the Second World

War. Numerous murders were being committed in the capital, but few of them were being properly investigated because of limited police resources. The war had also led to a lack of funding for forensic experts and, as a result, the use of its scientists seemed to take a huge backward step.

THE NEMESIS
OF SLAYERS

One of those cold-blooded wartime slayings in London involved a woman choked to death and dumped in the River Thames. After her body was recovered, she was examined by highly respected pathologist Sir Bernard Spilsbury. Spilsbury was renowned throughout the world of forensic science after inventing the "murder bag", which contained everything any forensic scientist could ever need when visiting a crime scene. Spilsbury had also shown the way when it came to gloves, bags and tweezers being used by all forensic experts to avoid contaminating evidence.

He later said he knew the woman had been murdered from the moment he looked into her eyes and realized from their blooded veins that she'd been strangled. Spilsbury also recognized the red dots on the skin as classic petechial (a minute reddish or purplish spot containing blood that appears in skin) marks. They were especially noticeable under the eyelids of the corpse, and they also proved that foul play had been involved in the death.

The wet conditions provided further clues, because this had caused Grave Wax – a crumbly, white substance – to be present on the face, breasts and buttocks of the corpse.

This and other sloppily investigated murders during the war years had a profound effect on Spilsbury's spirit, though. He was already reeling from the death of two of his closest relatives, and after performing more than 25,000 post-mortems he'd started to suffer from appalling bouts of depression. At around 8 p.m. on the evening of 17 December 1945, Spilsbury found himself alone with his thoughts at his laboratory inside the department of pharmacology at University College, in Gower Street, central London. It all proved too much for him. A few minutes later, the smell of gas was so strong that when a colleague of his passed his office he tried to open the door. Finding it locked, the man summoned the janitor, who, armed with a passkey, opened the door. Spilsbury lay slumped across his workbench, gas hissing from two unlit Bunsen burners. They tried to resuscitate him but to no avail. Less than an hour later, Spilsbury was pronounced dead at the scene. He was 70 years old.

Spilsbury's death – like his career – made big newspaper headlines. Ironically, his tragic end sparked more adoration and praise than perhaps he had ever enjoyed while he was alive. He was proclaimed across the globe as a forensic pioneer. The *New York Times* stated: "Britain has lost the nemesis of slayers. A man whose unrivalled knowledge and genius for deduction had made him a household name in criminal jurisprudence."

It seems that Spilsbury had made up his mind to end his life after a series of tragedies had rocked his family, and he was immovable from that decision. It was typical of a man

31

who controlled every aspect of his professional life with such precision. Some would say he was a dedicated scientist right to the end.

CRIME THRIVES

After the end of the war, Britain evolved into a grim place. The 1950s saw the nation's crime rate skyrocket. In London, gangs of professional criminals were taking over the streets of the capital. Many of these mobs used murder frequently as a warning to their enemies. The police struggled to get anyone in this chilling new underworld to help them to bring such killers to justice.

Certain police officers even ignored forensic scientists on some cases because they were in the pockets of criminals, who paid for many such investigations to "go away". Even some of the most honest police officers dismissed forensic scientists as getting in the way of their attempts to take the bad men off the streets because they took so long to analyze their findings about murders. One senior Scotland Yard detective said at the time: "It's all very well having those professors on tap but they're too bloody slow for my liking. In this game you need to get the bad boys locked up double quick. You can't hang around while some boffin in a white coat juggles test tubes for months on end."

Back in those unruly post-war days, some detectives rewrote criminals' statements and planted false evidence to secure convictions rather than waiting for the forensic experts to come up with something. Those types of officers saw nothing wrong with faking evidence, because they believed it was their "duty" to convict criminals by "any means necessary".

Scotland Yard Flying Squad chief Tommy Butler was a classic example of this mentality. He hated the forensic scientists most of the time and saw them as slowing down his own manic quest for justice. Yet, ironically, his biggest claim to fame – 1963's notorious Great Train Robbery – was solved in part thanks to a fingerprint found by forensics on a salt container at the farm where the gang hid out after the robbery. One officer from that era recently told me:

Tommy Butler fuckin' loathed the forensic boys. I remember one time he tried to get this nerdy type scientist fella to help plant a fingerprint in a bank, which had been robbed by a notorious gang of professional robbers. We all knew one particular crook had been involved in the job, so in our minds there was no harm in making sure he got arrested. But this forensic professor bloke went ballistic at Tommy for even suggesting such a thing. But not even this academic type would report it to the top brass at the yard because we all worked to the golden rule that you never grassed up your colleagues in those days, whatever they did and whoever you were. But Tommy Butler and that forensic fella never spoke to each other ever again.

Forensic scientists regularly walked away from investigations rather than do anything "unscientific". But a small minority did cave in to pressure from certain detectives and provide supposed evidence, which would be enough to enable the police to arrest a suspect. There were only a very small number of allegedly crooked forensic investigators, though. The majority were disgusted by the way crooked police officers tried to use them to put away their enemies.

This awkward attitude between the police and forensic scientists lasted until at least the mid-1970s. That's when law enforcement agencies were faced with some significant forensic developments, including a specialized method that could detect gunshot residue using a scanning electron microscope, and other sophisticated tests developed to examine saliva, semen, sweat and other body fluids.

At the same time there was another steep rise in violent crimes in the US and UK, especially murder. Criminal gangs were swapping bank robberies for drug deals on a huge scale. Narcotics were considered a lot less risky for professional villains than heists and security van hijacks. But with such vast earning potential, murders between gangs became much more frequent.

Also, there was the emergence of a chilling new type of criminal – the serial killer – who struck with impunity and in cold blood. They were opportunistic killers who nearly always had no direct connection to their victims. That meant traditional investigative skills were much less effective. Forensic evidence would clearly be a crucial aspect to solving any serial killing case. "Serial killers back then were like evil criminal ghosts drifting from town to town picking up people and murdering them with impunity," explained one retired Los Angeles homicide detective. "Serial killers would snatch people off the streets or stalk them for days without even being filmed on a CCTV camera. With no cell phones it would have been impossible to prove they had even been in a certain location."

Overstretched, underfunded police forces during this period found themselves out on a limb, unable to cope with such widespread death and destruction coming at them from both directions. As a result, random serial killers seemed destined to remain on the streets and never be brought to justice, while police pursued more traditional professional criminals.

The need for sophisticated, fully equipped forensic laboratories had never been more urgent. They would enable scientists to put their own unique stamp on investigations and earn the respect they thoroughly deserved. One young British scientist – who recognized the importance of intense research into unchartered areas of forensic science – set up a small laboratory inside a university in the centre of England, where he began work on something that would alter the face of crime investigation for ever.

DNA

This book goes out of its way to acknowledge many generations of forensic experts in all their glory, but there is one stand-out character whom many believe single-handedly changed the face of forensic science and law enforcement for ever.

In the late 1970s, Alec Jeffreys – born 9 January 1950 – was a young British geneticist, working as an up-and-coming professor at Leicester's prestigious Department of Genetics, in central England. Its pathology department eventually went on to be hailed as one of the world's foremost forensic facilities. Professor Jeffreys was quietly developing techniques for genetic fingerprinting and profiling, at a time when most people hadn't even heard of "DNA". Jeffreys ran his own small laboratory at Leicester University with one part-time technician. He was, however, given considerable freedom to experiment.

It was a time when technology was gradually emerging which enabled scientists to properly study genes. Jeffreys concentrated on the inherited variation of genes at first. When he felt he had them properly investigated, he switched his emphasis from products of genes, such as blood groups, to DNA. Deoxyribonucleic acid – or DNA, as it's better known

– is the main component of chromosomes. It carries genetic information of all forms of life.

In 1978, Jeffreys and his small team of one at Leicester University began working out how to detect variations in human DNA and started mapping genes in disease diagnosis. By 1981, Jeffreys had pledged to his Leicester University peers that his main goal was to distinguish highly variable strands of DNA. So he and his team looked even more closely at how these genetic variations evolved. Jeffreys tested out samples taken from his own lab technician before eventually uncovering the first inherited DNA variation. Jeffreys knew this was the key to what he was trying to do.

That's when he stumbled on what he later called "stuttered DNA", or "minisatellites". They turned out to be highly variable. He worked out a way to detect these numerous minisatellites. It became clear they were all variable enough to potentially provide their own uniquely informative genetic markers.

But it was early days yet, and Jeffreys knew he needed to continue his work on DNA in order to confirm the significance of his findings. So for the moment, he kept his research very low-key. Few outside the university even knew what he was working on.

COLD-BLOODED MURDER

Just five short miles away from Professor Jeffreys' laboratory at Leicester University, the chilling murder of a teenage schoolgirl had rocked the village of Enderby, in the heart of the English countryside. Police had discovered the body of 15-year-old Lynda Mann on a little-used footpath on the outskirts of the village on 21 November 1983. A post-mortem revealed that the teenager had been beaten, raped and strangled, and a semen sample from her attacker was retrieved from her body.

Detectives at the time were informed by their own forensic team that the suspect's blood group profile matched approximately 10 per cent of the UK's entire male population, and it was not practical to test millions of potential suspects. Initial police enquiries came up with a number of suspects, including one local man who was discounted after proving to detectives he'd been looking after his baby son at the time of the attack. Eventually the hunt for Lynda's killer went cold.

Back at his lab at nearby Leicester University, Professor Alec Jeffreys was using his DNA-based research work to primarily study hereditary diseases in families, because it seemed the best way to utilize what he already knew about the exclusivity of DNA. Jeffreys focused in on paternity and immigration disputes by demonstrating the genetic links between individuals through their DNA. He was trying to devise a system to help identify such people while studying X-ray images during a DNA experiment he was running in his lab when – at 9.05 a.m. on Monday 10 September 1984 – he stumbled on what was to become the world's first actual genetic fingerprint.

Jeffreys' initial response had been: "This is too complicated". But as he described it many years later, "the penny then dropped" and he realized the momentous scale of his forensic breakthrough. The key to Professor Jeffreys' discovery of DNA fingerprinting was that humans have remarkably little genetic diversity. There are about 20 million known Single Nucleotide Polymorphisms (SNPs) in the human genome. This means that the odds of someone having the same DNA by chance is like having a deck of 20 million cards, all different, and drawing the same three million cards in the same order twice. Jeffreys' DNA research conclusively proved that every person's individual DNA had its own profile and print. This would pave the way for a vast improvement in the ability of law enforcement to track down killers who left their DNA at the scene of murders, as well as many other serious crimes.

Jeffreys and his team quickly grasped the significance of their research and how it would impact crime, paternity and identical twins, as well as working on conservation and diversity among non-human species, plus the evolution of gene families, which can help spot genetically inherited medical ailments before they occur. The quietly spoken scientist also realized that what he'd stumbled upon even had a political dimension, because it had the potential to change the face of immigration disputes, especially when no documentary evidence existed.

Within six months of the discovery – as word of Jeffreys' unique work spread in the scientific world and beyond – he found himself being swamped with immigration cases. The first application was to save a young boy from being deported by proving his blood relationship to his mother. A paternity case soon followed, and the flood gates opened even further.

Up to this time, all cases were being dealt with inside the Leicester laboratory headed up by Jeffreys. As a research fellow for the Lister Institute, he received specific funding to employ another technician so that he could run more sophisticated tests on a larger scale. Jeffreys' laboratory remained the only one doing this type of research for the following two years. It was still considered a "work in progress" by many inside and outside the scientific world.

Professor Jeffreys believed by this stage that the half-life of DNA — the point at which half the bonds in a DNA molecule backbone would be broken — was 521 years. So, under ideal conditions, DNA evidence could last about 6.8 million years, after which time all that bonds it together will finally be broken.

Gradually, police forces across the UK started to hear about Professor Jeffreys' DNA fingerprint findings. They recognized that if this system worked, it could revolutionize law enforcement across the globe.

ANOTHER KILLING

In the summer of 1986, a second teenage girl living near Professor Jeffreys' laboratory at Leicester University set off on a journey she would never return from.

At 4.30 p.m. on Thursday 31 July 1986, 15-year-old schoolgirl Dawn Ashworth left a friend's house in the village of Narborough to walk home. Dawn lived in the nearby village of Enderby, where the body of Lynda Mann had been found three years earlier. It was just a few minutes' walk away.

The teenager chose to take a shortcut along a footpath known locally as Ten Pound Lane. After that, she vanished. Two days later, Dawn's body was found in the corner of a nearby field, covered in twigs, branches and torn-up nettles.

The pathologist who examined the body quickly established that Dawn had put up a considerable struggle before being raped and strangled. The police believed that they were looking for a serial killer, because not only did they now have semen samples from both victims, but Lynda's clothes had been removed in the same manner as Dawn's, and she too had been killed with her own scarf. Detectives believed that the killer had to be a local man, someone who knew the area, and possibly knew Lynda.

Narborough, Enderby and the surrounding villages became paralyzed with fear. One local newspaper warned: "If we don't catch him it could be your daughter next." The vicar of Enderby, Canon Alan Green, urged the murderer to give himself up, "because at some time in the future you will have to face your creator and account for the terrible thing you have done".

Initially police believed the rapist and murderer to be 17-year-old Narborough resident Richard Buckland, who appeared to have knowledge of Dawn's body and even admitted to the crime under questioning.

Buckland – who had learning difficulties – also knew Dawn. He seemed to know some details of the crime that had not been made public. Under questioning, he repeatedly admitted the murder to a detective, although he later withdrew that confession. On 10 August 1986, Buckland was charged with Dawn's murder, and appeared in court the following day.

But by this time Buckland was adamant that he was not guilty of murdering Dawn. The police – who knew that both girls' lives had been taken by the same person – remained convinced he was lying.

THE FIRST TEST

Following Richard Buckland's first court appearance, Professor Alec Jeffreys – already something of a local hero thanks to his now well-publicized work on DNA – received an unexpected call from the police, asking him whether his new scientific breakthrough could prove that the youth had murdered Lynda as well as Dawn.

Professor Jeffreys tested the semen recovered from both victims and concluded the same person had indeed committed both crimes. He then agreed to carry out DNA tests on Buckland's blood. He stayed up through the night to finish the work, recognizing the importance of proving the guilt of a suspected serial killer.

After removing the film from the developing tank in his laboratory, Jeffreys could see once again that the two girls had been raped by the same man – and that Buckland's DNA was completely different. He immediately told detectives that, although they were correct in their belief that one man had raped and murdered both girls, their suspect Buckland had not killed either of them.

The police were astonished and found it hard to accept they had been so wrong. Professor Jeffreys was asked to repeat the same tests again. When that came up with identical results, he was asked to do them all over again.

By this stage, the police were starting to regret ever getting a scientist involved in their precious double murder enquiry in the first place.

"One minute we got the guy," a local detective commented at the time, "and the next we've got Jack shit."

After a third round of identical tests, Professor Jeffreys assured detectives he was 100 per cent certain the results were conclusive. Innocent suspect Richard Buckland was released – after more than three months in custody – and the police were back to square one in their hunt for a cold-blooded double killer.

Richard Buckland became the first person exonerated thanks to Professor Jeffreys' new DNA fingerprinting system.

FINDING THE RIGHT MAN

Having recovered their composure after admitting they'd got the wrong man, Leicester detectives realized that this was an opportunity to use Professor Jeffreys' brand new technology to catch the killer of the two teenagers. Leicestershire Constabulary and forensic scientists agreed to join forces to organize testing the blood and saliva of 5,000 local men so their DNA could be compared with the suspect's DNA profile. In effect, they were going to screen the entire neighbourhood. It was an enormous undertaking but, armed with Professor Jeffreys' brand new DNA technology, they believed it would be worth it.

Initially, detectives targeted every male born between 1953 and 1970 who'd lived or worked in the Narborough area in recent years. Two testing centres were set up at a local school and a council office. Morning and afternoon testing sessions were held three days a week. Each man was also expected to bring proof of identity.

After six months and thousands of samples being taken, no match had been found. The police were understandably disappointed, and some officers began mumbling that perhaps the science hadn't been right after all.

It was pointed out to them that it was a voluntary scheme, which a considerable number of men had declined to take part in, claiming they did not like needles. Others refused to give samples after saying openly they didn't trust the police. When locals heard about these refusals, they made clear to all their fellow citizens the horror and disgust they felt about the double killings. Many still feared that the killer could strike again. As a result of this extra pressure, the original dissenters eventually started coming forward to be tested.

With increasing numbers of men providing samples, the forensic science laboratories conducting the tests struggled to keep up with the sheer volume.

Nearby, the killer of those two teenage schoolgirls believed that as long as he remained calm, he could still get away with his heinous crimes.

Meanwhile, in other parts of the world, the operation to catch a serial killer in Leicestershire was beginning to get a lot of attention. Many were hailing this as potentially one of the most significant breakthroughs in crime detection since fingerprinting was invented. But until police brought the killer of those two teenage girls to justice, a lot of observers still remained sceptical. Some even suggested that the failure to find the killer meant the entire DNA testing programme was clearly suffering from some kind of human error. There were even suggestions that the UK Parliament should outlaw any future mass screening programmes because they encroached on people's basic human rights and didn't work anyway.

Once again, the reality of the fear which had been struck into the community near where the murders had been committed meant that the majority of local citizens believed the police efforts to catch the killer were more important than any of the issues raised.

Eight long months later, a total of 5,511 men had given blood samples. Only one had actually refused. Yet there was still no match with the semen samples, so detectives expanded their hunt even further for the serial killer.

Among those recorded as providing a sample at this time was Colin Pitchfork, a 27-year-old baker and father of two young children. Three years earlier, he'd been questioned about his movements on the evening that Lynda Mann had been murdered. He'd told detectives, quite correctly, that he'd been looking after his young son.

In late June 1987, a local man called Ian Kelly told his mates at his local pub that he was paid £200 to provide police with a DNA sample for one of his friends, who happened to be Colin Pitchfork. Kelly openly admitted he'd impersonated Pitchfork, in order to take the blood test on his behalf. Kelly said that Pitchfork requested this favour after claiming he had already taken the test for another friend with a conviction for indecent exposure when he was younger. Pitchfork doctored his own passport by inserting Kelly's photograph in it so Kelly could show it at the test centre as proof of identity before he took the test. Pitchfork even drove Kelly to the test centre at the school and waited outside while the blood sample was taken.

Six weeks after Kelly's boast in the pub – in August 1987 – one of the people who'd been drinking with him relayed Kelly's conversation to a local policeman. Kelly was arrested and within hours Pitchfork was also in custody. DNA testing soon confirmed Pitchfork as the double killer.

After reading him his rights, a detective asked Pitchfork about his most recent victim. "Why Dawn Ashworth?" he asked. The killer shrugged his shoulders and replied: "Opportunity. She was there and I was there." Pitchfork provided police with a detailed confession to both murders and two other sexual assaults. He admitted that while he raped and killed Lynda Mann, his car had been parked nearby with his baby son asleep in the back of it.

Pitchfork eventually appeared at Leicester Crown Court and pleaded guilty to two counts of murder, two of rape, two of indecent assault and one count of conspiring to pervert the course of justice. He even admitted his fetish for flashing females, an impulse that had led to sexual assault and finally murder.

A psychiatric report read out in court recorded Pitchfork had a "personality disorder of psychopathic type accompanied by serious psychosexual pathology" and warned that Pitchfork "will obviously continue to be an extremely dangerous individual while the psychopathology continues". He was sentenced to life imprisonment and set a minimum term of 30 years.

While Prof Jeffreys' work saved innocent Richard Buckland from suffering a serious miscarriage of justice, Pitchfork's guilty pleas in court meant that the DNA evidence was not specifically needed by the prosecution. This was significant because it meant this new science had not yet been comprehensively tested as pivotal evidence in a court of law, although it was clear the DNA fingerprint tests originated through Professor Jeffreys' research work had huge investigative potential for police forces around the globe. In the UK, others recognized that this DNA system could soon be incorporated routinely into police casework and numerous technicians and forensic scientists began to be trained to handle DNA in preparation for the "gold rush".

Within a couple of years, DNA testing kits were incorporated into most law enforcement detection equipment, and

Professor Jeffreys was being hailed as a scientific genius. Jeffreys himself was soon to become known as the father of genetic fingerprinting. In 1994 he was knighted by the Queen for services to science and technology. And the DNA fingerprinting "monster" he'd stumbled on in a laboratory in Leicester was going from strength to strength.

DNA DATABASES

Today, DNA fingerprinting is acknowledged as having single-handedly brought about the biggest change ever seen in the world's criminal justice system. It helps solve crimes, identify the victims and can even link a single event to other offences. Samples of DNA taken at a crime scene are examined through genetic records on a database for a DNA match. A "cold hit" is when a person is flagged up who may well be responsible.

In the early days of DNA, police in the UK, US, Australia, Canada, France, Germany, the Netherlands and elsewhere organized DNA dragnets to try and track down suspects, and then developed their own individual DNA databases. It's reckoned that more than 50 million people worldwide have – over the last 30 years – had their DNA tested during criminal investigations.

That is estimated to have helped secure the convictions of at least a million criminals. It's also helped innocent suspects find justice and overturn miscarriages of justice.

These days, police can extract DNA samples from suspects much more easily than in the early years of its development. Sometimes suspects are simply followed until they discard a soft drink can or even a tissue if they don't volunteer for a test. In the UK, the world's first national DNA database was established in 1995. It currently contains the DNA profiles of 5.8 million people taken from 5.1 million people. That is the equivalent of almost 8 per cent of the population. Recently in the UK, many samples were removed from the DNA database after it was found that those profiles had been taken from people who were not convicted of a crime.

Upon receipt of a DNA match from within the UK's National DNA Database, the police will often proceed to arrest the suspect, although they're rarely charged on the basis of a DNA profile match alone – appropriate supporting evidence is usually required.

In the US, the FBI has developed something called the Combined DNA Index System (Codis). This contains a DNA database which holds nearly 14 million offender and arrestee profiles. It's also seen as a vital tool for helping link local crimes to offenders outside those jurisdictions. Another important function of DNA in criminal cases is enabling the victims of crime to be identified, even if a body is unrecognizable.

If the same DNA is found at two different crime scenes, it can be used to link a suspect to other offences. This allows criminal investigators to determine if a serial criminal is at large or to establish if the victims knew one another, and this doesn't just involve murders, either. Officers and forensic scientists in countries including the UK and US are today at pains to point out that anyone involved in a sexually moti-vated attack is likely to one day have a knock on his or her door, thanks to DNA fingerprinting.

One former London serious crimes detective explained: "I hope the people who think they've got away with these sorts of crimes, however long ago, are now haunted by how DNA and the latest other investigative techniques will one day bring them to justice – because they will." Another former London police officer explained: "Until DNA fingerprints came on the scene, most people who got away with their crimes at the time of the offence no doubt presumed they'd never be brought to justice. But they're wrong. We can come and get those offenders any place any time."

FAMILIAL DNA

At the end of the 1990s, a new type of ultra-sensitive DNA testing system was developed. It was initially known as Short Tandem Repeat and was based around retaining genetic profiles on complete families rather than just individuals. Today it's more commonly known as familial DNA, and it has helped solve many cases going back decades.

This system can match up specific repeating patterns in DNA, which helps identify profiles to an incredibly narrow degree so that a sample can even be matched to the relative of a suspect. Familial DNA was first pioneered in the UK by the Forensic Intelligence Bureau, which was in the early 2000s part of the government-run Forensic Science Service. The FIB had its own bureau of six forensic specialists dealing exclusively with cases through the use of familial DNA.

The key to the process was to re-test samples and spread out the potential for DNA matches by covering entire families. The development of familial DNA was handled sensitively, as it involved using the relatives of suspects to try and bring killers and other serious criminals to justice.

DNA TRANSFER

DNA transfer – the migration of cells from person to person, and between people and objects – is inevitable when we touch, speak, or even do the basic household chores. One recent study showed that sperm cells from a single stain on one item of clothing could end up on every other item of clothing in the washer. That means even the strongest DNA profile on an object doesn't always correspond to the person who most recently touched it.

You can pick up a knife at 10 in the morning. But a forensic analyst testing the handle later that same day could well find a stronger and more complete DNA profile from a person who'd used the knife four nights earlier. It's even possible that forensic analysts could find a profile of someone who never touched the knife at all.

In another study, participants were asked to shake hands with a partner for two minutes and then hold a knife. When the DNA on the knives was examined, the partner was identified as a contributor in 85 per cent of cases, and in 15 per cent as the main or sole contributor.

That means DNA transfer can be relatively random. The mere presence of DNA at a crime scene can completely distort the truth and sometimes condemn innocent people for crimes they had no involvement in whatsoever.

Homeless Lukis Anderson had a long rap sheet of non-violent crimes, which meant he had submitted his DNA to the US database. In November 2012, murder squad detectives in California found Anderson's DNA at the scene of the cold-blooded killing of millionaire Raveesh Kumra at his mansion in the foothills outside San Jose, near San Francisco. Forensic experts had matched biological matter found under victim Kumra's fingernails to Anderson's DNA database.

Anderson was held in jail for a total of five months before his lawyer was able to produce records showing that his client had been in detox at a local hospital at the time of the killing. Later it emerged that the paramedics who'd originally responded to the emergency distress call from murder victim Kumra's mansion after he was found had treated Anderson earlier that night. They had inadvertently transferred his DNA to the crime scene via an oxygen-monitoring device which had been placed on Kumra's hand.

FALSE POSITIVE
DNA MATCHES

One of the most basic questions in genetic genealogy is whether a matching DNA segment is "large enough" to investigate further. Small segments of matching DNA can show a very slight match, which is completely irrelevant to the DNA found at the scene of a crime. The police themselves are not always sufficiently knowledgeable when it comes to DNA samples to appreciate this. These are called false positive DNA matches, and the risks of them occurring are highest if a DNA test result is held in a large database containing millions of details.

In 1999, 49-year-old Raymond Easton from Swindon, in the UK, was arrested and charged with a burglary in a town more than a hundred miles away from his home. A DNA sample taken from the crime scene matched Mr Easton's DNA profile on the UK national DNA database. Despite being in the advanced stages of Parkinson's disease and unable to walk more than 10 metres without help, he was kept in custody until his lawyer persuaded police to run further DNA tests, which immediately exonerated him.

It only later emerged that Mr Easton's DNA profile had been loaded onto the database four years earlier following a domestic dispute, and the police "match" to his DNA being at the scene of the crime was actually 37-million-to-one, but this was not highlighted enough by the computer programme testing the sample.

As this case so cruelly reveals, DNA matches do not automatically confirm the identity of an offender. And it's likely that there are other innocent men and women languishing in prisons in the UK and elsewhere in the world, who've been found guilty of crimes they simply did not commit. "Just classifying it as a 'false positive match' doesn't tackle the problem in any way," one former murder squad detective said. "DNA is not always right and the police particularly need to appreciate this much more than they currently do."

NEW DNA
TECHNOLOGY

It's believed that in the very near future DNA samples will enable investigators to create actual descriptions of potential suspects. This is down to the latest, fast-developing spin-off from DNA, called DNA phenotyping. This involves predicting an organism's features using only genetic information collected from genotyping or DNA sequencing. A description is built through a mathematical model that can eventually predict actual appearances.

DNA phenotyping will not only be able to predict physical appearances from DNA, but scientists also claim it could be used to provide vital leads in criminal cases where there are no suspects or database hits. It will also help to narrow down lists of suspects, as well as providing more results from the examination of human remains, which could lead to breakthroughs in cases. One scientific research company has already begun accurately predicting the physical appearance of an unknown person by adapting their DNA sample. This include skin, eye and hair colour, plus freckles, ancestry and even face shape.

But, for the moment, DNA phenotyping raises more questions than it answers due to the questionable accuracy of the technology, particularly when it comes to recreating facial images. Other critics fear that this new development in forensic science might lead to increased racial profiling within law enforcement agencies, which would undoubtedly infringe on an individual's privacy, as well as encouraging racial stereotyping.

In the middle of all this, DNA itself continues to be developed and utilized away from the crime-solving marketplace. Today, numerous spin-offs are emerging, including the development of new medicines and even new food types.

In China, scientists even claim to have created the first-ever gene-edited twin baby girls. They're said to have altered the DNA of the babies in order to ensure they were not susceptible to genetic diseases. The twins – called Lulu and Nana – represent a profound leap of science and ethics. This type of gene editing is banned in most countries as the technology is still experimental and clearly highly controversial. There are also fears that using DNA to develop future generations of people could have unforeseen and chilling side-effects, as it is one step nearer to a future world where people are chosen before they're even conceived.

Meanwhile, DNA has been used in other, more understandable ways. Recently, forensic scientists were able to prove that skeletal remains uncovered in a burial pit in Yekaterinburg, 850 miles east of Moscow, were those of Russia's last tsar,

Nicholas II, and his wife and children. They'd all been killed in 1918, during the Russian civil war. DNA matches were made with samples taken from several people related to the family, including the Queen's husband, the Duke of Edinburgh.

FIBRE TRANSFER

It's not just DNA which has revolutionized forensic science, though. Experts have developed tests that can detect increasingly minute particles linking murder victims to their killers.

Every time someone puts on a coat, hugs somebody or sits on a sofa, tiny little fibres from their clothing will be left behind. Individuals can also pick up similar fibres left on those same objects by other people. This is known as fibre transfer, and forensic scientists now test for it all the time to solve crimes. As a result, textile fibres have become one of the most important types of evidence available to a forensic examiner.

The key to this type of forensic work is not the fibre itself but how it came to get where it was found in the first place. Until recently, it had been presumed that fibre transfer only occurred when two surfaces touched, like when a jumper touches the shirt of someone else. That is now known not to be the case. Fibres can be transferred in other ways, too. Forensics call this "contactless airborne transfer". It's when fibres move from one garment to another without contact. This means two people can be in the same room, not even touching each other, and the fibres of one person's clothing can transfer through the air to the other person present.

A typical example would be two people who were in an elevator when one allegedly assaulted the other. If hundreds of the victim's fibres are found on the suspect's clothing, it's highly unlikely that contactless transfer alone is the reason for all those fibres. If only a few fibres are found, contactless transfer is most likely to be the case.

Contactless airborne transfers eventually played a significant role in solving the murder of at least five prostitutes in the east of England in late 2006. Paula Clennell, 24, Anneli Alderton, 24, Gemma Adams, 25, Annette Nicholls, 29, and Tania Nicol, 19, were all killed between 30 October and 10 December that year. DNA was found on all the victims. It matched up to a local forklift truck driver called Steven Wright, whose DNA was in the UK database because he'd once been arrested for theft.

But as well as the DNA, red acrylic fragments were found on the back seat and parcel shelf of Wright's car which were indistinguishable from microscopic material found on the bodies of victims Miss Alderton, Miss Clennell and Miss Adams. Fibres from a tracksuit worn by Wright at the time of his arrest were found on the bodies of Miss Alderton, Miss Nicholls, Miss Clennell and Miss Nicol, as well as other fibres from his home in Ipswich, Suffolk.

Other fibres found in the hair of Miss Adams – whose body was discovered in a brook – had been transferred through "forceful direct contact", according to a forensic scientist giving evidence at Wright's eventual trial. There was clear evidence that victim Miss Nicol had been subjected to "forceful or prolonged" contact with items from Mr Wright's home, car and clothing around the time of her disappearance.

Only tiny remnants of the original fibres deposited on the bodies of all five victims were uncovered by forensic experts, because the majority of material had been washed off the bodies as a result of how they'd been dumped and left exposed to the elements. Two of the victims had been found in water, which made the recovery of evidence by forensic scientists all the more extraordinary.

One forensic expert assured the jury during Wright's trial at Ipswich Crown Court that the transferral of fibres "would not have occurred by chance".

Wright's defence team claimed that he'd used all the women for sex, but that that didn't prove he'd murdered them.

Wright was found guilty of all five murders on 21 February 2008. The following day, he was sentenced to life imprisonment, and the judge recommended that he should never be released. If serial killer Steven Wright had committed those murders 25 years earlier, he would most likely have got away with the killings, because airborne transfer of fibres and DNA was not detectable back in those days.

FORENSIC ECOLOGY

There are many sides to forensic science, but one of the most remarkable developments in recent years has come through the experts who can trace natural evidence at a crime scene and even on a corpse. They are the forensic ecologists. Their role is to find and analyze substances such as grains of pollen, spores of plants, fungi, lichens and microorganisms.

One such specialist is Professor Patricia Wiltshire, known to some by a particularly graphic nickname – the "Snot Lady" – because of her ability to recover pollen grains even from the nasal cavities of the dead. Professor Wiltshire's findings often provide murder investigators with crucial evidence of what happened during a death, thanks to those microscopic fragments. She's usually called upon after none of the traditional forensic evidence, such as fingerprints, DNA and fibre, have been recovered at crime scenes.

One forensic scientist explained: "These days the police and others tend to expect DNA and other forensic clues to exist at every murder scene but this isn't always the case, so you need a plan B and that's where people like Professor Wiltshire come in." Forensic ecologists are expected to dust themselves down and get on with looking for other, less obvious evidence, because it's always there somewhere. As one of them explained: "You just need to take the time to find it."

Professor Wiltshire and others in her field are hunting for evidence that is nearly always invisible to the human eye. As a forensic ecologist, she operates in a no man's land between the criminal and the natural world.

Professor Wiltshire describes the human body as being a mass of beautifully balanced ecosystems – even after death. She recently explained: "Your dead body is a rich and vibrant paradise for microbes. Nature is marking us on every step we take."

SOLVING A PUZZLE

The discovery of a mummified corpse in a sports bag on the side of a busy road in Yorkshire by two teenage boys proved a huge challenge for Professor Wiltshire. There was no clue as to the identity of the victim, except that the remains were male. Apart from for the lower legs and feet, the body was wrapped in airtight, see-through cling film.

An initial forensic autopsy showed that the man had been stabbed, but the pathologist who examined the remains could not ascertain how long he'd been dead. However, there was one yellow sycamore leaf stuck to the thigh of the corpse. Also – from the shins down – the skin of the victim was covered with a black sooty material which Professor Wiltshire realized was a thick mass of fungal spores, which had grown over the body after death. She quickly deduced that the body had been kept in an unkempt garden with plenty of rose-type pollen, as well as clematis and the pollen of sycamore, pine, and birch trees.

Professor Wiltshire noticed some sand stuck to the skin on the back and front of the torso, as well as in his hair. Following an online facial reconstruction comparison, the man was discovered to be a Yemeni immigrant. His home and family in Yorkshire were located, and the police who arrived at the house to inform relatives of the tragic discovery couldn't help noticing the garden was very similar to the one described by Professor Wiltshire. She travelled to the victim's house and soon spotted the remains of an old clematis plant straggled over a fence next to some roses. There was also a sycamore tree in the garden.

That single leaf had managed to preserve enough evidence to establish an accurate picture of the place, which helped detectives unravel the case.

Investigators' next move was to enter the cellar of the same property. There they found clear signs of a recently dug hole where the body must have been buried originally. It also contained particles of sand that matched the samples found stuck to the victim's skin.

This proved the final piece in the puzzle for detectives. The victim's son and grandson confessed to being involved in the killing but insisted there were mitigating circumstances. The suspects painted a picture of a cruel old man whom his son and grandson could not tolerate anymore. When the old man put a knife in a fire and deliberately burned his grandson's leg with the blade, they grabbed the knife from him and stabbed him with it. The father and son were eventually tried on manslaughter charges but received relatively light sentences after sympathy shown by the court and police.

FINDING A BODY

Professor Wiltshire's unique skills have also helped find missing bodies at the centre of murder enquiries. When Joanne Nelson vanished on Valentine's Day in 2005 from her home in Hull, in the north of England, her boyfriend Paul Dyson initially told the world she'd run away. But after 11 days of sticking to his story, he confessed to strangling Joanne after she'd nagged him to do some household chores.

The police now had their man. But there was one big problem – no body.

Dyson told detectives that on the night he'd murdered Joanne, he wrapped her body in plastic and drove her in his Vauxhall estate car far into the Yorkshire countryside north of Hull. Eventually, he stumbled on a lonely spot and buried her. Now, almost two weeks after the murder, he couldn't remember where that location was. He told bemused police officers it could have been anywhere that required less than half a tank of petrol to reach. That included a vast area of Yorkshire, which was too big for police to properly cover.

Professor Wiltshire immediately focused on Dyson's car, because she believed she could tell from pollen grains, spores and other microscopic particulates where that vehicle had travelled. After painstakingly conducting her analysis,

Professor Wiltshire informed police that Joanne's body was most likely not buried under the ground at all. She'd deduced this from pollen found on the car which showed the sort of terrain it had travelled through. Professor Wiltshire even told detectives that the remains would most likely be covered with birch twig litter.

With those clues and killer Dyson's co-operation, police were eventually able to find the location of the body. It was exactly as Professor Wiltshire had predicted: out in the open in an isolated woodland dip near Hovingham, in North Yorkshire.

Paul Dyson pleaded guilty to murdering Joanne Nelson and he was sentenced to life in prison at the end of his trial in November 2005. As Professor Wiltshire later explained: "It doesn't matter where we go in nature, we always leave a trail behind us, and I used these clues to point police in the right direction."

PSYCHOLOGICAL
FOOTPRINT

The majority of forensic scientific techniques rely mainly on physical evidence, but there is another approach to murder cases that can provide investigators with genuine, significant breakthroughs. This involves psychological assessment of what's going on in a suspect's head in order to try and come up with vital, tangible evidence that will help detectives to apprehend a criminal and even secure a conviction.

Unsurprisingly, trying to work out the identity of a killer and what has driven that person to commit murder and carry out sex crimes is a complex process.

Forensic psychologists have to dig deep to find out what is going on in the human brain, and this is when they work best, alongside police officers, in order to profile criminals. One UK forensic psychologist explained: "The key to all this is knowing why some people commit crimes and others don't. It means trying to get beneath the surface of people's person-alities, which is especially hard when it comes to criminals. By nature, they like to hide most stuff."

Many forensic psychologists admit that common sense often plays a huge role in helping them to understand a case, especially if they are brought in after a crime – often murder – has been committed but before a suspect has been apprehended. "This can prove particularly useful when there is no obvious suspect," explained one recently retired London murder squad detective:

> We have nothing to lose and I've been astonished over the years how accurate forensic psychologists often turn out to be. They seem to be able to use crime scene evidence and geographical positions of crimes to build a picture of a suspect. A lot of my colleagues used to ignore this sort of stuff. I learned over the years that every suspect – even the ones we don't know about – leaves a psychological footprint behind them, even if there is no physical evidence of who they are.

One of the key indicators of an offender's identity obviously revolves around the type of crime they are alleged to have committed, as well as the way it happened and a timeline of everything that led up to the crime and its subsequent aftermath. This can result in a profile that can turn out to be a remarkably accurate description of a suspect.

Many forensic psychiatrists believe that personality disorders are the root cause of most serious offences, especially murder and rape. Often, these perpetrators have earlier committed other less deadly crimes. Forensic psychiatrists have discovered through their work that many of the worst types of killers and rapists often were stalkers and voyeurs when they were younger.

One forensic expert explained: "We can read a lot into who these characters are through the past as well as the present. So often there is a behavioural trail that leads from someone's childhood all the way to the crime they have committed. The nervous systems of some killers is different from the rest of the population because they can't get a thrill from the sort of things normal people would. That's what often leads to subversive behaviour such as voyeurism and stalking during their teenage years. It is our job to map out how they came to develop from those crimes into murderers."

THE FORENSIC
SCIENCE SERVICE

All the staff inside forensic laboratories across the world know that their work potentially makes the difference between a killer being caught or remaining undetected, which could well lead to an offender going on to kill again. As one forensic scientist explained: "That's the part of our job that hardly ever gets a mention. We feel a great weight of responsibility for what might happen in the future if we miss something. A killer could go free and go on to murder more people and that's down to us. It's a heavy cross to bear."

The UK's Forensic Science Service began life as a network of regional forensic science labs back in the 1930s. In 1996 the Metropolitan Police's laboratory in Lambeth, south London, was taken over by the FSS, which at that time assumed complete control of forensic services throughout the UK. The FSS became England and Wales' largest employer of forensic scientists. The service came under the aegis of the UK Home Office. In Scotland, the responsibility fell to specific police forces. In Northern Ireland, the regional government ran it. But the vast majority of FSS employees were paid out of the coffers of their respective police forces.

By 2000, the FSS was processing around 90,000 cases a year and regularly dealt with incidents of murder, sexual assault, burglary, drugs and firearms.

As scientific techniques continued to evolve, the FSS began using a process called Low Copy Number (LCN) testing when it came to DNA samples. This involved taking a minuscule sample of DNA from clothing or other items and amplifying them to get a DNA profile.

The FSS was also the only forensic organization in the UK at that time to have developed what has become known as "Cinderella analysis", thanks to its own unique database of shoe prints. Scientists could actually work out who the regular wearer of a specific shoe was by using information such as the angle of footfall and weight distribution. The FSS also built its own comprehensive database of soil from around Britain, which eventually held more than 10,000 samples. This could help place an individual at a crime scene or eliminate them from an enquiry altogether.

However, in 2003 – just seven years after the FSS took over the UK's forensic system – the Labour government under Tony Blair announced it was paring back the organization in a cost-cutting exercise. Ministers encouraged UK police forces to begin contracting out their forensic work to private companies, which were rapidly launching into the marketplace. The UK government believed at the time that this move would help create a highly competitive marketplace and that forensic costs would be driven down to provide better value for money. But many British forensic scientists were appalled by the move because they considered their scientific work too important to be simply sent out to tender.

In 2011, three FSS laboratories were closed in an attempt to balance the books following a £50 million government bail-out two years earlier. At this time, the FSS still accounted for 65 per cent of the UK's "forensics market", with the remaining 35 per cent taken up by companies in the private sector. In 2012, the new Conservative government announced the FSS would be completely closed down. Home Office minister James Brokenshire claimed that the service was losing £2 million a month. He stated it was "uncompetitive by charging too much for its services and consequently losing business to commercial rivals".

One London forensic scientist commented: "It was akin to telling criminals they had a free reign to do what the hell they wanted because the police no longer had some of the tools they needed to solve crimes."

As a result of the FSS closure, some of the UK's foremost forensic scientists moved abroad, where salaries were higher and jobs were considered more secure than they were in London and other British cities. "Those cutbacks and the closure of the FSS sparked a mini-brain drain," explained one London forensic scientist. "It felt like we were being pushed out of the way in a cost-cutting exercise, which completely ignored the need for our services when it comes to solving crimes."

Meanwhile, the UK police continued their drive to cut budgets and costs. This resulted in them becoming over-focused on DNA evidence to the exclusion of key corrobo-rative branches of forensic science, ranging from weapons examination to finger printing. One forensic scientist told me recently: "It was an appalling situation. We were scientists trying to solve deaths and we found ourselves in the middle of bidding wars where private forensic companies were under-cutting each other to get work. The police were even asking forensic labs for quotes and dropping entire investigations because they couldn't afford the fees being quoted. In other words, crime investigations were being shelved purely for financial reasons. Not good."

* * *

In TV dramas such as *Silent Witness*, most murder myster-ies are wrapped up in a few hours of screen time. In reality, forensic investigators can take weeks, months and even years trying to extract crucial evidence connected to an unsolved murder. Forensic scientists and law enforcement person-nel always have to dig deep to find the motive for murder. It can't all be simply deduced from one sample of DNA. Finding that evidence, turning it into something tangible and using it to bring the guilty to justice is a complex process, as all the elements have to fall into place after a murder investigation is completed.

All forensic investigators are continually looking for basic physical evidence. This can be any item that eventually links a suspect to a crime scene. That could mean, for example, identifying a fibre retrieved at a murder scene belonging to an Armani jacket, or that a bullet had been fired from a Glock G24 pistol.

Forensic science wouldn't work at all if it wasn't for the different and varying disciplines of numerous highly skilled individuals. In real life, cases tend to be solved in segments. That requires patience and dedication. Everyone from scene of crime officers to specialist forensic scientists has their own role to play. Information is always carefully collated, and that is often encapsulated in a carefully worded report, which can be backed up by later appearances in court by an expert witness.

Forensic experts examine everything in the aftermath of a death, from forensic odontology (the identification of unknown human remains through dental records and teeth marks) to anthropology (the study of skeletal or fragmentary remains in order to create a biological profile) to basic pathology. Experiments are often repeated over and over again, and such time-consuming hard work is a key component when it comes to helping solve serious crimes, especially murders.

THE LABORATORY OF THE
GOVERNMENT CHEMIST

As a result of the closure of the FSS organization, there are today numerous privately run forensic crime laboratories around the UK. What was once the FSS's "jewel in the crown" facility in Lambeth is now a privately run laboratory which, in fairness, continues to be a highly innovative forensic facility.

These days, the private-equity-financed former Laboratory of the Government Chemist (now named the LGC Group) is Britain's largest single supplier of outsourced forensic science services. It employs 675 forensic scientists across 8 laboratories in the UK. Two hundred and twenty-five of them are based at their main laboratory on a former RAF base in deepest Oxfordshire, England. This place is eerily similar to *Silent Witness*'s Lyell Centre in many ways and specializes in chemical and biological traces, as well as DNA, plus a wide range of other forensic research services.

The labs within the LGC's main building in Oxfordshire run off a vast, long corridor, and the overriding theme is blue. It's mostly spotlessly clean and there is little sign of wear and tear. Every set of swing doors contains security keypads. On the doors are bright red and yellow notices:

No Entry for Unauthorised Personnel.

Danger, Hazardous Materials.

Approved Clothing Must Be Worn.

The most dramatic notice of all is:

Stop! DNA Sensitive Area. Do Not Enter Unless
You Have Given An Elimination Sample.

Beyond the swing doors are technicians in hairnets, face masks, scrubs, lab coats, and two pairs of latex gloves – one long, blue and pulled up over coat cuffs; the second short, flesh-coloured and changed with great frequency.

All exhibits from crime scenes arrive and are immediately and carefully logged. Depending on the type of case and the nature of the evidence, an appropriate senior scientist is allocated to oversee each job. All this evidence has already been meticulously documented at a crime scene, where it is known as the "Chain of Custody" process. The miniscule clues found during close inspection of every inch of a crime scene include hairs, fibres and latent fingerprints, which are often not visible to the naked eye. All evidence is then tested and stored in the presence of a video camera, which is done to avoid any of it being dismissed as inadmissible evidence in a court of law.

One of the first tests inside the LGC's Oxfordshire lab is for fingerprints. These have a unique pattern of loops, arches and whirls that belongs to each individual. Visible prints can be seen on a surface such as blood or dirt because they leave a proper impression. Those have ridge characteristics, which are the matching patterns of fingerprints which help identify a specific person. The key element is the loops and whirls of each print.

But there are also latent prints. They can be found on various surfaces, from a piece of glass to an actual murder weapon, or anything else that the perpetrator has touched. Often they can't be seen with the naked eye, but have to be uncovered using dark powder, lasers or other light sources. In the US, the FBI have their own patented Advanced Fingerprint Identification Technology (AFIT) which even uses an algorithm to improve fingerprint match accuracy.

At the LGC laboratory, tests are then carried out to analyze all bodily fluids.

To test for semen, forensic technicians usually use acid phosphatase, an enzyme that is itself found in semen. If the test turns purple within a minute, it's positive for semen. To re-confirm such findings, technicians also examine slides of a semen sample under a microscope. That's when the colours of the heads of the sperm appear red and the tails green. As a result, that test is referred to as the "Christmas tree stain".

Traces of blood invisible to the naked eye are located in the LGC lab with a Kastle-Meyer test. This uses a colourless substance, phenolphthalein – which turns pink in the presence of blood – to test for blood and can involve technicians scratching at barely visible stains of blood with small paper pads in order to extract blood for this "KM screening".

Another test for blood is luminal, which is often sprayed around a murder location to detect even the tiniest droplets of blood but can be used in the laboratory as well. These tests often follow an analysis of blood splatter patterns found on the surfaces of a crime scene. These can provide vital evidence for forensic investigators because they can show if a weapon has been used, as well as the wound size and type of injury sustained.

In order to detect even the tiniest amount of saliva found at a crime scene, the LGC lab uses a highly specialized test to detect amylase, an enzyme found in human saliva. If amylase is present, a blue dye is released which means saliva is present and traceable.

Next come impact marks. These are often an essential piece of potential evidence for forensic investigators. Impact marks can be found on any surface or a recovered object, however small. This can help provide technicians with essential information, especially when it comes to investigating shooting-related cases.

Among the most common causes of deaths investigated by forensic scientists are hit-and-run vehicle cases. In the LGC lab, a typical physical examination involves comparing a paint sample found on the body of a hit-and-run victim with a make and model of car. The LGC lab and other crime investigation facilities use advanced equipment to study what is very often an extremely small and seriously damaged sample. Often the scientist looks at the colour, thickness and texture of it under a polarized light microscope to view its different layers.

Another crucial test in the LGC laboratory will be a weapons analysis. When a gun is fired, its residue exits the gun behind the bullet. Forensic investigators look for gunshot residue on a suspect or victim's hands or clothing, although some weapons don't discharge it. Police usually use special tape or a swab to lift residue off the hands of a suspect, and those samples are part of the evidence that is closely examined at the LGC facility. Forensics technicians at the LGC lab use a scanning electron microscope to examine such samples. Elements in gunpowder have a unique X-ray signature, so they will flag up under examination.

Spent bullets are also examined for striations. These are the marks that match the unique patterns inside the barrel of a gun. Technicians also use dithiooxamide (DTO) and sodium rhodizonate – known as the Greiss test – to detect the presence of chemicals produced when a gun is fired. This is an analytical chemistry test which can determine the presence of nitrates, a common component that is found in all explosives and gunpowder.

Establishing the type of weapon used during a knife assault involves a similar type of process in some ways. Scientists will closely study the width, depth and shape of a cut, as well as the edges of a wound, which can prove if a smooth, serrated or irregular surface caused the injury.

Narcotics tests are increasingly relevant in murder cases, as the use of pharmaceutical and recreational drugs is today believed to be relevant in more than 50 per cent of all sudden deaths. The LGC laboratory usually tests for drugs through a microcrystalline test. A technician will add a drop of a suspected narcotic substance onto a chemical on a slide. This forms crystals. Each type of drug has its own crystal pattern, which can be seen under a polarized light microscope.

Also used for narcotics testing at the LGC lab is gas chromatography, which can isolate any drug from mixing agents or anything it has been combined with. Molecules can move through the chromatograph's column at different speeds based on their density. How the substance breaks apart can help the technicians tell what type of substance it is.

Arson is another hard-to-solve crime that forensic technicians at the LGC lab investigate with great care and attention. Most deliberate fires are started with a flammable material and an accelerant such as kerosene or petrol.

One of the key aspects of this type of investigation is the ability of forensic scientists attending the crime scene to recover any containers that might have held the accelerant. They often have latent fingerprints on them. Such containers are invariably found dumped nearby or at a suspect's house or in a relevant vehicle. More often than not, there is little else to examine at the scenes of arsons, other than charred remains. But once they are expertly packed up and transported back to the LGC lab for analysis, technicians can more carefully examine all the evidence.

Many technicians inside the main LGC lab in Oxfordshire sit at desks covered with brown paper upon which lies evidence that can range from those charred remains of items to clothing like sweatshirts, jeans and trainers.

These technicians use strips of clear tape to pat gently on items repeatedly in order to lift off fibres.

Tucked well away from natural light, other forensic examiners toil away in the Marks and Traces Laboratory, located within the main laboratory building. At first sight, it looks like a well-equipped school lab, with 10 rows of benches.

Each bench contains a computer screen, microscope and sheets of brown wrapping paper covering lumpen shapes. These shapes are "bagged" evidence taken from crime scenes throughout the UK. The paper is used to help stop contamination.

At the far end of the room, a forensic scientist hunches over a trainer being held steadily under a fluorescent strip light fixed from the ceiling. The investigator dusts the shoe with aluminium powder before holding it against an acetate sheet in order to take an imprint of the sole. This will be matched against imprints taken from the scene of the crime. Next to that investigator, a car wheel and tyre rest upright and untended. On another bench close by, an acetate sheet bears the imprint of a shoe sole from another unsolved crime.

Inside LGC's DNA Unit, scientists can search for DNA in everything from blood to brick dust. Two scientists are at work, wearing obligatory white lab coats, hair covers, face masks and gloves. Only approved personnel are allowed inside this sterile environment. Anyone entering has to carry out a deep clean because of the risk of contamination. This is done to ensure that all those present can be eliminated from any cross-contaminated DNA samples.

The LGC's DNA Unit within the Oxfordshire lab building contains two £120,000 Hamilton Microlab Starplus Robots. These form the central core of the lab's automated DNA examination centre and they can extract DNA from even the smallest samples before quantifying and measuring the DNA material within them.

Next door to this is the Grim Room. Its full title is the "Glass Refractive Index Measurement Room". Glass fragments from suspects' clothes, hair and the rest of the body can be compared here to "control" fragments from a crime scene. These are examined under a microscope. A sample of those fragments is placed in a special oil before being warmed up and cooled down until the fragment refracts light at the same point as the oil. The glass itself "disappears" into the oil. The sample is recovered in the light at the same point. This means both samples of glass are likely to be from the same source. These types of results are frequently used to corroborate DNA evidence, as well as wider police investigations. So this can often greatly contribute to bringing a case to a satisfactory conclusion.

Managing each examination inside the LGC lab building is a reporter, who liaises with the police and works out a strategy to use in order to maximize the chances of obtaining results from the available material within a reasonable space of time. He or she plays a role in keeping costs to a minimum relative to the importance of the specific case. These reporters are in many ways the "managers" who help to weld all these forensic specialists together. They write up statements on behalf of the forensic scientists for the police. They liaise between departments and they mend any broken fences, as well as encouraging team spirit between all departments.

LGC even runs a "call out" service, providing experts for crime scenes at very short notice. This includes firearms specialists, who can help identify weapons and ammunition, and a digital forensics team, who will gather evidence from devices such as computers and phones.

Today, the LGC is at the forefront of recent advances in digital and computer-led forensic science, including the use of specific computer programs to, for example, predict where a criminal lives based on the location of crimes that he/she has committed.

But forensic science isn't always just about murder and other violent, cold-blooded crimes, in the usually accepted term of the phrase.

THE IAIN WEST
FORENSIC SUITE

Pre-eminent forensic scientists such as the previously mentioned Dr Iain West are as renowned for their handling of disasters as murder mysteries. These types of cases often involve
multiple deaths and provide investigators with completely
different challenges from traditional homicides.

When Dr West died prematurely of cancer in July 2001
aged just 57, many in the forensic world felt it was apt to
name a brand new facility after him because it had a unique
capacity to handle vast numbers of bodies.

The Iain West Forensic Suite – which cost almost a
million pounds to build – was constructed next to central
London's Horseferry Road Police Station and was opened
in 2008, just seven years after West's death. Not even *Silent
Witness*'s fictional, high-tech Lyell Centre forensic laboratory
could match this specialist morgue's capacity for handling a
vast number of bodies for examination at any one time.

The suite was specifically designed to be used exclusively
for post-mortem examinations of suspicious deaths. It was the
biggest of its kind in the world when it was opened. The facility could deal with mass casualties and had the space to store

up to 102 bodies. There was even a bio-hazard post-mortem room with a CCTV viewing area that is similar in some ways to *Silent Witness*'s Lyell Centre version.

The Iain West Forensic Suite itself is attached to the Westminster Public Mortuary, which deals with around 600 deaths per year. It even has mobile X-ray machines which can reveal and track the trajectory of bullets.

The forensic suite came into its own in June 2017 following the Grenfell disaster in west London, when a residential tower block was destroyed by fire. This turned out to have been the worst residential fire in the UK since the end of the Second World War. A total of seventy-two residents died, plus two deaths in the hospital, of a child and one stillbirth.

One prominent London forensic scientist explained:

> Iain West would have been tailor-made for the Grenfell investigation because he was fearless when it came to investigating these types of disasters and making far-reaching conclusions. He was also well used to dealing with multiple numbers of bodies and seemed to take it all in his stride. Dr West's attitude would no doubt have been that it could have been avoided and he would have recommended all sorts of measures to try and prevent any similar disasters from happening.

Forensic scientists played a crucial role in the identification of Grenfell victims, as well as working as on-the-ground investigators probing for a cause for the blaze. All the Grenfell victims underwent post-mortem computed tomography (PMCT) imaging using a mortuary-based mobile scanner based at the UK's legendary forensic facility at the East Midlands Forensic Pathology Unit inside Leicester University. But instead of having to transport all the bodies of the victims there, the scanner was deployed remotely from the Iain West Suite to the radiology team at the University of Leicester more than one hundred miles away. This minimized the number of personnel necessary in the mortuary because space was limited. And the Leicester team of forensic technicians were able to conduct their examinations remotely while still having eyes on the remains at the same time.

A remote reporting system for mortuary scanning was used to speed up the process, which meant 119 corpses were scanned during an 18-day period at a rate of 18 per day. This process would have taken at least twice that length of time if each body had had to be transported to Leicester.

Each body and its relevant paperwork had to be brought to the scanner to be recorded by dedicated body movement police officers inside the Iain West suite. All body bags had to be scanned in their entirety to ensure any loose fragments in the bags were also recorded. When each scan was completed, an INTERPOL number was assigned to the body to help with future identification. It was a monumental task on a scale rarely seen in the UK. As the radiographers were scanning and signing paperwork, body movement officers completed the register of each victim. Two DVDs of the scanning data were recorded for police evidence after completion of each scan.

The size of this forensic operation was unprecedented. A team of four investigators, with three support staff members, managed to provide full radiology reports for the forensic teams at the Iain West Suite within one working day of each scanner image being received.

As one London forensic scientist explained:

This was forensic science at its most basic but that large number of bodies needed to be properly examined in an orderly fashion and there are not many places in the world where that can happen. Dealing with so many victims stretched the suite's facilities to the maximum. But they were able to handle it and it's important to highlight this side of forensic science, just as much as the murders and suchlike. Just imagine what it must have been like for the examiners and officials inside that mortuary as the bodies literally piled up. Yet they achieved everything they set out to do and no stone was left unturned.

Another forensic scientist remarked: "Around the world, other forensic scientists looked on with fascination and a bit of envy because the efficiency of the process for the Grenfell investigation was mind-blowing. The technicians managed to cut the time factor in half and when you have such a sensitive case involving a high number of victims, that makes everyone's life easier and more productive."

As of September 2020, the Grenfell fire is still being investigated by the police and a public enquiry team, and coroners' inquests remain outstanding. The main issues include the management of the building itself by Kensington and Chelsea London Borough Council. There were questions about the responses of the London Fire Brigade on the night of the blaze and subsequently. There is no doubt that forensic investigations carried out in The Iain West Forensic Suite will contribute greatly to the eventual conclusions of all the parties looking at the Grenfell fire.

Across the UK and in some other countries, local governments have investigated other tower blocks to find out if they have similar exterior cladding, which has been blamed for causing the Grenfell blaze to have spread so quickly. Efforts to replace the cladding on these buildings are ongoing. However, without facilities like the Iain West Forensic Suite, it would be even harder to deal with the multiple victims of these types of disasters.

THE BODY FARM

DNA was by no means the only significant development within the world of forensic science over the past 50 years. Many forensic scientists have used their enthusiasm and knowledge to become innovators, and their ideas have helped solve numerous murders and other crime mysteries.

The characters behind these and other developments in forensics are rarely acknowledged outside the scientific establishment because of the sensitive nature and public response to those who "work with the dead". Not all these innovations are developed in a traditional laboratory, either. Forensic scientists sometimes work out of unique facilities that are specifically created to deal with some of the most basic elements of forensic science. This is where practical research is needed in order to improve the investigative skills of the experts.

On a scrubby, rundown, abandoned plot of fenced-off land in the countryside just outside South Knoxville, in Tennessee, lies one of the most important forensic facilities in the world. For on these barren fields and among the shabby outhouses is a unique anthropology research centre, which contains more secrets of the dead than probably anywhere else in the world. It generates data on tissue and bone degradation under controlled conditions. It also allows for chemical changes in the soil, air and water around a corpse, which helps forensic scientists to establish the location of a murder or serious crime with much more ease.

This place is commonly called "The Body Farm", although others have somewhat flippantly dubbed it a chilling, surreal "theme park for the dead", in recognition of Hollywood horror films like *Night of the Living Dead*. Body farms are better known in the world of forensic science as forensic cemeteries or taphonomy facilities, after the discipline devoted to the study of decay and fossilization.

In one corner of this land, the remains of what appears to be a body sit in an abandoned vehicle. In another area, a corpse has been buried just beneath the surface of the ground to replicate the way investigators believe the person was killed. But these dead bodies are not models from a movie set. They're real corpses who're giving up secrets which may eventually lead to the arrest and conviction of their killers. It's said the wind is never strong in these parts, which is just as well because if a strong gust came through here some of those old bones would be sure to be disturbed.

World-renowned forensic anthropologist William Bass opened this outdoor facility back in 1981, specifically to study how human bodies decompose. Many believe that it has since helped revolutionize certain areas of forensic research. Not surprisingly, it's a bizarre place where the dead literally dominate the surroundings. The Body Farm's specially donated human remains are decaying in "controlled environments" which Bass and his team of forensic scientists believe will help investigators to work out the fate of crime victims.

Dr Bass set it all up in the belief that it would enable investigators to unravel the truth about why bodies decompose in differing circumstances and what they can tell scientists about everything from time of death to the reasons behind why a death occurred. The facility was inspired by American bone collections dating back to the nineteenth century, although those human bones are of no use to today's forensic researchers. Bodies have changed in the past 100 to 150 years due to diet and general standards of living. So modern skeletons are vital to today's Body Farm. More than one hundred corpses are donated to the facility every year. Some individuals pre-register before their own death. Other bodies are donated by their families or a medical examiner.

The facility itself helps to train law enforcement officers to deal with many of the disturbing situations they might find through their jobs. It's especially helpful to young, rookie cops unused to dealing with dead bodies, because it normalizes their attitude towards a corpse. This enables them to properly address all the relevant issues that so often occur at a death scene.

"It's a fantastic way to 'harden up' a police officer's ability to deal with a dead body, which is something they all have to endure regularly throughout their careers," explained one forensic scientist.

Most "inhabitants" of William Bass's Body Farm usually become so decomposed that only their bones remain, and that is the crucial condition for Bass and his researchers. It takes an average of two years for those corpses to end up being a skeleton. These remains are cleaned, recorded and carefully labelled before being officially "enrolled" into this unique facility for the dead.

It takes at least a day to do this properly once all the skin has shed. That usually entails an anthropology student using water and a toothbrush-like brush to clean dirt and tiny bits of tissue off bones. If any of those bones retain mummified tissue, they're warmed in slow cookers or large kettles, which are just hot enough for the remaining tissue to be pulled off them with tweezers or cut with scissors. It's essential that the bones are not boiled, as that could damage any DNA. Orthopaedic equipment such as artificial knees or hips remain with the bones in their boxes. Hands and feet are placed in soft cloth bags, and teeth and tiny bones or cartilage kept in small boxes.

The skeleton box itself is made of cardboard and just 8 inches high, 10 inches wide and 3½ feet long. Bones go – long bones first – into the box according to an accompanying diagram. The skull sits in its own divided compartment.

Internal medical implements such as pacemakers, stents or pumps which are not attached to bones are stored separately. Those devices often bleep eerily every 10 minutes from their boxes.

The boxes containing these remains are stored on floor-to-ceiling, electronically controlled shelves in what is called the W. M. Bass Donated Skeletal Collection inside a special unit at Tennessee State University's Strong Hall. It's all part of the university's Forensic Anthropology Center, overseen by Bill Bass himself. With some 1,600 skeletons and room for more, the Bass Donated Skeletal Collection is the largest collection of individuals' bones for medical research in the United States.

New batches of skeletons arrive regularly in the state-of-the-art classroom/laboratory building. It's entered by a locked wooden door that looks from the outside like an ordinary office entrance. Meanwhile, researchers and scientists regularly attend the nearby Body Farm to study what those bones can tell them. Their findings relate to fields including biology, forensics, anthropology, dentistry, genetics and biomedicine. But these bones don't just help scientists to solve murders. They can provide clues as to how different diseases or illnesses affect bones. University forensic anthropologists use some of the same skeletons for essential training sessions. The remains come from victims of a wide range of crimes and accidents, including shooting victims complete with bullets still in the body, and a car crash victim who might happen to have a healed fracture uncovered by forensic scientists examining remains.

At the centre of all this death and destruction are the families of the deceased who donated their bodies, many of whom visit the Body Farm regularly. At least a dozen relatives come each year. One woman who has visited the bones of her cousin several times explained that being at the Body Farm provided her with a mixture of science and comfort. "It doesn't feel morbid or sad," she insisted.

Most of the families who visit the Body Farm meet the scientists to discuss forensic anthropology and how and why their relative's remains are being used in research or training. Some even request a viewing of their relative's bones. That's when scientists including Dr Bass talk to them and explain about the intricate side of the science. Many families are initially unsure but eventually come away happy to have donated their families' bodies. On a few occasions, relatives have even been known to ask to see the bones taken out of their box and arranged as a skeleton on a table covered in protective padding.

One forensic scientist who's visited the Body Farm explained: "One of the most impressive aspects of the facility is the brilliant way they deal with the relatives of the dead. Everything is done with the utmost respect and patience." The same scientist recalled that he came away convinced that every family was proud that their loved one had ended up contributing to such imperative forensic science questions.

And the demographics of the corpses at the Body Farm is fascinating. The majority of skeletons – about two-thirds – are those of white men, and most of them are from inside the Tennessee area and tend to be in their fifties. But there are other relatively young and extremely old remains, which apparently surprises many who visit the Body Farm. This includes a 16-year-old, as well as the remains of a 101-year-old man. Less well known is the fact that this facility houses the bodies of cremated, unpulverized remains and a small collection of infant skeletons. This includes a small collection of infant and still-birth skeletons, from 20 weeks' gestation to two months old.

Since opening the Body Farm in the early 1980s, Dr Bass has helped solve dozens of cases. But one of them perfectly illustrates why his facility is so crucial to forensic science, whatever the eventual outcome of a case.

LEOMA PATTERSON

Back in 1978, 56-year-old Leoma Patterson left a bar in Clinton, Tennessee, never to be seen again. She literally disappeared into thin air. Six months later, a female skeleton was discovered in a wood on the edge of a lake in a neighbouring county. The bones found buried in the ground seemed to match the missing woman, and one of Patterson's daughters recognized a ring found at the death scene as belonging to her mother. But it wasn't until six years later that a relative of Patterson's – one of the men she was last seen alive with – confessed to killing her. It seemed to be an open-and-shut case in the end, although other relatives of Patterson's were not convinced he'd done it.

In 2005, those same relatives persuaded Dr Bass to re-examine the disputed remains and collect DNA samples, which could not have been done at the time of the prosecution. It would turn out to be a murder case that would test his knowledge of forensic anthropology. In the end, Dr Bass turned to mitochondrial DNA testing to determine if Leoma

Patterson was really in the grave, because it was much more sensitive than the usual DNA tests. A sample was eventually extracted from the skeleton and compared to the DNA of two of Leoma's daughters. The DNA did not come back as a match. The chapter ended with Dr Bass bringing back the bones to the lab to figure out who had been buried in Leoma's grave.

Unfortunately, the secrets of a corpse don't always reveal the comfortable truth, and no one to this day knows what became of Leoma Patterson's corpse, or who those bones belonged to.

THE UK BODY FARM

In the UK, forensic scientists are currently working alongside the British military to construct a similar Body Farm-type facility to the one opened all those decades ago by Dr Bill Bass. Many inside the world of forensic science say this UK-based version is long overdue. Details about the UK body farm are top secret for sensitivity reasons, but law enforcement sources say that work first started in late 2019 to develop this unique research facility.

In the summer of 2020, rumours emerged that the UK Body Farm was being located on land close to the UK defence ministry's most well-known scientific site, the Defence Science and Technology Laboratory at Porton Down, near the city of Salisbury, in southern England. This long-standing facility analyzes everything from chemical weapons to poisons to viruses. Porton Down even hosts training sessions for "cadaver dogs" to find human corpses, and has in recent years invested heavily in purchasing adjoining land for new laboratory space. It's claimed this land is where the body farm is being developed.

The new body farm site was put on ice for at least six months following the coronavirus outbreak in the early months of 2020. The facility is expected to be opened by the end of 2021.

UK forensic scientists insist that such a facility would undoubtedly provide crucial information to criminal investigations that can't be obtained from one-off studies which are only connected to specific cases. However, a small minority of UK scientists and police have dubbed the planned facility as "gruesome" and claim that the value to scientific and forensic research is minimal. "There are some people out there who see a body farm as some kind of Frankenstein-type project," said one prominent UK forensic expert. "Nothing could be further from the truth. Such a place could only help, not hinder, unsolved murders and other serious crimes."

Meanwhile – as Britain wrestled with the sensitive issues revolving around such a facility – it emerged in 2020 that at least six more Body Farm sites were to be opened in the United States. In recent years, forensic researchers have set up similar facilities in Australia, the Netherlands and Canada.

DEALING WITH
THE DEAD

But what about the human cost for forensic scientists them-selves, whose professional lives are so closely aligned to the dead? Many I've spoken to openly acknowledge that their job involves certain sacrifices when it comes to their private lives and health. Some have talked openly about the bizarre triggers that remind them of their work and how that can play tricks with their minds at the most unlikely moments. One distinguished forensic scientist once told me: "We're not machines. We're human beings with hearts and souls and sometimes all this death and destruction can have a devas-tating effect on our mental health." Many such scientists admit that often the details of their first few cases rest the most heavily on their minds.

Most outside the forensic world tend to presume that once a body is laid out in a laboratory it becomes nothing more than a slab of dead meat to scientists, enabling them to step back emotionally and do their job. But that's not the case at all. "Those first few cases can have a profound effect on you," one forensic scientist told me:

Your attitude towards so much stuff revolves around the early ones. They're supposed to teach you to close down emotionally but sometimes you can't help but be affected and sometimes it's hard to come back from that mentality. We're not cold, detached people. We often feel the same level of disgust, sadness and even anger as anyone else but we're not at liberty to show that. The truth of the matter is that many of the people we examine should never have died in the first place. That makes it doubly hard. There is always this feeling that it's another life wasted. The senselessness of so many deaths is hard to handle because you know you're looking at the body of someone who should still be alive and enjoying their life.

In the words of one world-famous forensic scientist who spoke to me:

I rarely let my guard down when it comes to my work. It doesn't install confidence in your colleagues if you start blubbering at the sight of a dead body. But I've never forgotten the first murder victim. She was a teenage prostitute found stabbed to death in a forest. She left a young baby. I remember looking down at her and feeling immense sadness because that girl suffered so badly at the hands of her killer. And there was the child she'd left behind. That girl has never left me. She drives me on with my job in many ways because every time I start to wonder why I'm doing this, I remember how cruelly her life was cut short and how my work helps get the killers off the streets, so that others who could have been victims will be saved.

So it's no surprise that forensic scientists suffer from disturbingly graphic nightmares which can even sometimes impact on their families. Another forensic scientist told me: "My own nightmares nearly always seem to revolve around hands. You often have to remove them to help speed up identification issues. This is rarely discussed publicly because it's something we try to keep quiet out of sensitivity for families of the deceased. But it's a brutal moment when you remove them. It feels as if you are removing part of who they are and that can be hard to come to terms with."

Today many pathologists believe that after particularly harrowing cases such as mass disasters, serial killings and spree shootings, forensic scientists should be given a psychological debrief as a matter of course, which is the case with most other emergency services personnel. The reason why this doesn't happen will surprise many. The majority of forensic scientists are self-employed, so they simply do not qualify.

"It's ironic that we're the ones left to our own devices to cope with such graphic and disturbing encounters with the dead," said one scientist:

But it's isn't just about our freelance status, either. It often feels as if everyone else involved in the process of investigating a death believes we're these tough, emotionally detached characters who're prepared to cut up people's remains without giving it a moment's thought. Nothing could be further from the truth. We don't just chop up body parts for the hell of it. In fact, many of us take great care to make sure a corpse does not look horrendous after we've done our investigations, however intricate they may be. We know full well that these people have loved ones and they deserve respect even in death. Remember much of this type of work takes place before relatives and friends of the deceased have a final moment to say goodbye.

Many of the forensic scientists I have spoken to want this "other side" to what they do to be publicly acknowledged, but all of them agree that ultimately the most important objective of all is to find out the truth. "The truth is what lies at the heart of everything we do," said one forensic scientist:

It drives us forward and fuels our work beyond doubt. Without that quest we don't have a goal. We often have to literally dig deep to establish why and how someone died. But that truth can come in many different shapes and sizes. Our job is not just about bringing murderers to justice, either. We also recognize that the victim's loved ones need to be given a true understanding of what someone went through before their death. Obviously we cannot bring someone back from the dead but we can explain everything in order to help the families understand what happened. It's a vital part of the process of grieving. If you don't know, it leaves a massive hole in your life emotionally.

Another forensic scientist explained: "Families and close friends of the deceased often want to know if their loved ones went through pain before they died. I always try to give them the truth because if they ever found out later that I'd sugar-coated what happened, that would be far more unforgiveable than simply providing the truth." When the injuries involved in a death are of an especially horrific nature it obviously makes this task much harder to deal with.

One forensic scientist told me: "Every case is unique but there is no doubt that some are tougher to handle than others. I struggle with any case that involves more than one simultaneous death. To have two or more corpses laid out in the lab and knowing they died together is much more difficult to come to terms with. To know that these innocent people are lying there extinguished of their lives because of another human being intent on killing them is mind-blowing. Although of course I usually keep those sorts of thoughts to myself."

One forensic scientist I interviewed for this book admitted that he frequently found himself at home with his family thinking in graphic terms about a murder he was dealing with at work. He explained: "I try so hard not to bring my job home but inevitably it seeps into everything, even though most of my colleagues claim they can switch off. How can you 100 per cent switch off from some of the scenes of carnage we have to face and smile with your family? It's not easy." Another forensic scientist I recently met told me how he sometimes has flashbacks to the remains of car crash victims, just as he is about to cross a busy road with his family. "It can be hard to cope with. In some ways I suppose it's like a warning 'system' to be careful but it often startles me and makes me nervous. Believe me, I really don't want those images invading my home life." So, in summary, forensic scientists are human beings like the rest of us.

THE
REAL
CASES

*The scene is the silent witness. The victim can't
tell us what happened, the suspect probably isn't
going to tell us what happened, so we need to give a
hypothesis that explains what has taken place.*

PETER ARNOLD, CRIME SCENE INVESTIGATOR (CSI) FOR THE
YORKSHIRE AND HUMBERSIDE SCIENTIFIC SUPPORT SERVICES

SOLVING MYSTERIES

This book has so far unravelled the technical facts, the personnel and the intricate practices of forensic scientists as they try to leave no stone unturned in their quest for the truth. However, there have been a number of high-profile cases in which the pivotal role of forensic scientists has until now been kept very much out of the public eye. These specialists played an unheralded role in trying to bring these cases to a satisfactory conclusion.

None of the dozens of forensic facilities across Britain would be in business today if it weren't for these murder mysteries, which scientists worked so hard to solve. They include other extraordinary breakthrough cases, which show why these experts now play such a crucial role in law enforcement across the globe.

"The more unusual a case, the more you can learn from it," explained one veteran forensic scientist. "My profession needs these sorts of challenges in order to improve our abilities as scientific investigators." Today, forensic scientists thrive on data and research from such cases to improve their knowledge of crimes. But what happens when someone dies in such unusual circumstances that there are no precedents?

GEORGI MARKOV

The first time I realized the importance of forensic science came following the death in London of a Bulgarian dissident called Georgi Markov back in 1978.

Markov – a novelist and playwright from Bulgaria – had relocated to England and was living in London working as a journalist and broadcaster for the BBC World Service. He was a stern public critic of Bulgaria's Stalinist regime.

On 7 September 1978, Markov was waiting near Waterloo Bridge in London to catch a bus when he suddenly felt a sharp pain in the back of his leg, similar to an insect bite. A man seemed to have accidentally poked him with his umbrella as he walked past. The stranger – later described as being heavy-set and speaking with a foreign accent – immediately apologized and briskly walked on.

Markov later that day recalled the incident to a colleague and his wife but thought nothing of it. That same evening, he collapsed and was hospitalized, suffering from severe sickness and a fever. By the following morning, Markov had a high fever, rapid pulse and low blood pressure. His wound was severely inflamed, and his white blood cell count soared. X-rays of his leg revealed nothing, and despite large doses of antibiotics, his condition worsened during the next two days. Markov told doctors about the pain in his leg and claimed he must have been poisoned by some kind of toxic dart. No one took much notice of what he said, but three days later he died at the age of just 49.

Scotland Yard ordered an autopsy to be conducted on Markov's body. During that examination, a section of the skin around Markov's wound was removed and sent to Dr David Gall, an expert in poisons based at the top-secret government Chemical Defence Establishment, at Porton Down, in the west of England.

Gall found a metal pellet the size of a pinhead with two tiny holes drilled into it. It was clear that something – containing a lethal substance – had been injected into Markov by a gas gun hidden in his assailant's umbrella. Inside the wound that had been caused by the umbrella being jabbed into his leg was a minute 1.52 mm pellet. It was composed of 90 per cent platinum and 10 per cent iridium, with two tiny 0.35 mm holes drilled through it.

The nature of Markov's demise made bacterial and viral entities unlikely culprits and strongly suggested a chemical toxin had been used. Only ricin, a substance derived from castor beans, seemed to fit the bill. But there was no reliable test for ricin available in the UK at the time. In any case, the body's natural enzyme systems quickly break down ricin, leaving no trace of it, which is precisely why it is one of the most effective and deadly poisons in existence.

So, in an ingenious experiment, forensic pathologist Dr Rufus Crompton injected an amount of ricin equal to what the pellet found in Markov could hold into a live pig. The animal quickly became ill and died in less than 24 hours. An autopsy of the pig showed organ damage identical to that in Markov's organs, suggesting that ricin was indeed the agent injected into him. Dr Crompton later explained: "The clever thing about ricin is that it mimics symptoms and appears in hospital investigations as natural disease."

Markov's attacker was never conclusively identified, though the Bulgarian secret police and Soviet KGB were blamed, particularly since they had apparently attempted and failed to kill Markov twice before in the past.

Some time later it emerged he'd been murdered on the orders of Todor Zhivkov, who was the Communist dictator of Bulgaria for 35 years. His rule tolerated no dissent, and writers had to toe the party line and sing its praises. Markov had even been sentenced in absentia to six-and-a-half years in prison for his defection to the UK some years previously. KGB defectors Oleg Kalugin and Oleg Gordievsky later confirmed that the KGB arranged the murder at the request of the Bulgarian Secret Service, whose agent, Francesco Gullino, used the weapon on Markov when he "bumped" into him on Waterloo Bridge.

After his death, Markov's works were withdrawn from circulation in Bulgaria, and his name was banned from being mentioned by their media until after the fall of Communism in 1989.

Just four short years later, a completely different kind of murder rocked London and has haunted the world of forensic science ever since.

ROBERTO CALVI

So-called "open-and-shut" cases are supposed to be the ones that cause few headaches for forensic scientists and police alike. Most suicides are classic examples of this, but some-times those hasty verdicts can haunt forensic investigators for decades and lead to extraordinary revelations that can turn an entire case on its head.

This occurred when I was a young rookie reporter in the early 1980s. I was one of the first journalists on the scene after a man's corpse was found dangling from a nylon rope tied to scaffolding underneath the centre of London's Blackfriars Bridge, one of the UK capital's most iconic ancient bridges. It was 18 June 1982.

At first, I couldn't quite believe what I was seeing. Just a few minutes earlier, I'd been sitting in the newsroom of the *Mail on Sunday* newspaper about to get myself an early morning coffee. One of my colleagues walked in breathlessly and said there was a body hanging from the bridge just 250 yards from our office. As a keen young reporter, it was a no-brainer. Myself and another journalist virtually ran to the scene.

The thing I remember most from that day was the bright orange nylon rope tied to scaffolding under the 200-year-old bridge. I could see it clearly from the moment I crossed the busy embankment running alongside the river. I remember thinking that whoever had staged this disturbing scene wanted the entire world to know what had happened to this man.

As I watched from the pavement along the north side of the river, I pulled out my notebook and began writing down the details. The victim was dressed in a grey suit with a white waistcoat and a blue striped shirt. I even noticed he was wearing expensive-looking shoes with leather soles and dark-coloured socks but didn't have a tie on and, I later discovered, no belt, either.

Reports said an expensive watch on his wrist had stopped at 1.52 a.m., just over six hours earlier. There were two heavy pieces of concrete stuffed in his clothing, which helped explain the weirdly stretched appearance of the clothed body as it hung there almost like a real-life version of the classic modern masterpiece painting *The Scream*.

Police who attended this grisly scene found a wallet in the victim's jacket pocket containing around £10,000 in various currencies, including Italian lire, Austrian schillings, US dollars and Swiss francs – and a passport bearing the name Gian Roberto Calvini. The passport turned out to be a forgery and the corpse was identified as 62-year-old Roberto Calvi, president of the Milan-based Banco Ambrosiano, one of Italy's largest banks with close ties to the Vatican. In the days following, Calvi's nickname of "God's banker" leaked out and it was revealed he'd gone missing from Italy just a week earlier.

Naturally, I knew little of this while I watched with morbid fascination as three young police constables struggled almost comically to take his body down from its bizarre and gruesome resting place. If this death had occurred more recently, I have no doubt the body would have been left in situ so that forensics could examine him exactly as he died.

But why and how this millionaire banker came to die was to become an international mystery that would take many of the world's most distinguished forensic scientists literally decades to try and solve. The Calvi case is one of the most talked-about killings inside the world of forensics. I've met numerous scientists down the years who are fascinated by this particular death and who consider its unravelling as the ultimate challenge.

The theatrical way the body was positioned, combined with the sinister forces who backed and opposed banker victim Roberto Calvi, made it a unique crime, more akin to a murder in a detective novel than reality. I remember standing on the pavement on the edge of the River Thames transfixed by the empty scaffolding creaking in the wind coming off the river after those young police constables had clumsily removed Calvi's body. I was convinced there was no way this man could have simply strung himself up.

Investigating the early stages of the Calvi mystery had a profound effect on my own future. It convinced me that crime was the area I wanted to report on more than any other, even though I didn't realize the full significance of this particular death in those early hours following the discovery of the corpse.

The Calvi story eventually turned out to have it all, with a backstory centred around the Vatican, Freemasons and organized crime. The location of the death – Blackfriars Bridge – had strong historical connections to the UK's most powerful Masonic lodge in the nearby City of London. In Italy, the Masonic lodge P2 had been known for years as Italy's shadow government. Members of P2 referred to themselves as *frati neri* – "black friars".

Calvi himself headed up a bank that was supposed to be a risk-averse institution. It had been founded in 1896 to offer credit and bank services to only those with supposed Christian ethics and beliefs. At one stage, the bank required anyone who wanted to use its services to first provide a baptismal certificate. In the first few days following that grisly discovery in June 1982, police investigators and forensic scientists presumed Roberto Calvi had succumbed to the pressures of his job and simply killed himself in gloriously public circumstances.

Dozens of police officers and paramedics invaded the crime scene on Blackfriars Bridge within hours of Calvi's death, and there is absolutely no doubt that they contaminated many of the most important clues, albeit accidentally. Today, that entire area would have been properly cordoned off and the bridge itself would have been closed, even though this would have caused chaos for the dozens of commuter trains which crossed it every hour on busy weekdays. As one forensic scientist explained: "There would have been no need for reconstruction of the crime scene because we would have insisted everything was left as it was at the time Calvi's body was hung there. I have no doubt significant clues would soon have been discovered but there was never that opportunity."

Instead, the entire scene was dismantled within hours of the body being taken down and transported to the local morgue where police and scientists rapidly completed all their forensic tests and examinations. They proclaimed it was just another suicide, albeit a very elaborate one. The London inquest held five weeks after Calvi's death confirmed that he had taken his own life.

His widow Clara and the couple's son Carlo immediately issued public statements saying the proceedings had been rushed through. They accused the police of not doing their job properly, especially in the first few crucial hours and days following the discovery of the body.

A second inquest was eventually held the following year, but it added to the confusion by returning an open verdict. This didn't mean Calvi had been definitely murdered, but it did at least concede that there were unusual circumstances surrounding the death of the man now dubbed by the media as "God's Banker".

It wasn't until 10 years later that the truth began to emerge, thanks to the combined efforts of at least three of the UK's leading forensic scientists, who offered their services free of charge in order to try and solve one of London's most bizarre murder mysteries. This new team of scientists decided to take a much more proactive approach than their forensic predecessors on the case in an effort to try and establish more scientific facts about the banker's death. They not only planned to re-examine all the evidence taken from the scene of Calvi's death but also closely studied items belonging to him that were found in the London flat he was staying at. The intention was to provide a full timeline of Calvi's movements by interpreting that information and combining the forensic evidence already available to the scientists.

Added pressure to get to the bottom of this mystery continued to come from Calvi's family, who remained extremely unhappy about previous inquest verdicts because, a decade after the banker's death, they'd become even more convinced he'd been murdered. Families are often the last ones to know about a loved one's suicidal intentions. But even Scotland Yard admitted in private before the new forensic examination that murder was looking more likely, although they were reluctant to talk openly about it until the scientists had completed their re-examination of the case.

First of all, this specially assembled forensic team had, as a matter of urgency, to reconstruct the actual death scene, which had been so recklessly dismantled immediately after Calvi's death.

Forensic scientists can only reconstruct what they actually know about a death scene. But even this can help them to work out the sequence of events which led to a death. That includes knowing where someone was standing when they died or were killed. This helps scientists establish what weapon was used, as well as how specific injuries were caused. The reconstruction can also provide forensic examiners with what is known as the "path of evidence", so they can work out where everything was located at the time the crime was committed.

More than a decade after Calvi's death, one member of the forensic team found herself directing her husband – also a forensic scientist – as he teetered on the exact same scaffolding that Italian banker Roberto Calvi had been found hanging on beneath the bridge. Only this time, it was erected in the garden of a bungalow in Newbury, Berkshire, in the heart of middle England. The husband and wife forensic team had been urged by the Calvi family to leave no stone unturned in an effort to get to the bottom of how the victim really died. As one of those scientists later explained: "The challenge was to minimise the variables so you are left with the version nearest the truth."

This painstaking experiment eventually proved that Calvi could not have hung himself from the scaffolding because the lack of paint and rust on his shoes proved that he had not walked on the scaffolding. The forensic scientist "playing the role" of Roberto Calvi even put pieces of concrete in his trousers to re-enact the last fatal moments before his alleged "suicide". The scientist suffered chaffing to his thighs from the weight of the concrete, but Calvi's body had no such marks. Similarly, the scaffolding poles left iron filings on the shoes and hands of the forensic specialist, but nothing was found on the dead man.

Forensic investigators also helped to uncover new evidence about the night before Calvi died. The contents of his stomach showed that he'd enjoyed a meal of pasta and beans in a restaurant near his flat in Chelsea, west London, where he'd been staying before planning to leave London to begin a new life with his family in the United States just a few days later. After leaving the restaurant, Calvi apparently walked the short distance to the north bank of the River Thames, where he boarded a boat for a twilight pleasure cruise. He'd allegedly arranged the trip earlier that same day.

A few minutes later, Calvi was standing on that boat when his killer is alleged to have come up behind him and placed the orange rope around his neck. His assassin garrotted him, pulling the cord with such force that he lifted his victim into the air. As Calvi struggled, his feet dragged along the deck, leaving deep scrape marks on the heels of his shoes. Markings and damage to the vertebrae in Calvi's neck suggested there were two points of strangulation, which further implied that other people were directly involved in his death.

The new forensic science team working on the case speculated that sometime after midnight on 18 June, Calvi's lifeless body was taken to Blackfriars Bridge, where the orange rope was tied into a lover's knot and placed around his neck. His killers were the ones who dropped two lumps of concrete in the trousers of the financier's grey suit, along with the cash that was later found on his body. The rope was tied to some scaffolding already on the bridge and the body was allowed to slip into the water. At the time, it was high tide, but by the early hours of the morning the water had retreated, and that's how the body came to be seen hanging from a steel pole.

The experts announced that scientific and medical evidence conclusively proved it was not suicide. The police suspected the Mafia carried out the hit. Many Italian mobsters had chosen London to live in during the early 1980s because they had a vice-like grip on the capital's lucrative cocaine market. As a result, there were a number of mafia bosses living in the UK capital. It was considered a more "discreet" place for an execution than back in Calvi's home city of Milan. Following the eventual publication of a report in 2002 by that new team of forensic scientists, a new City of London police enquiry was set up and his insurance policy was finally settled.

Detectives eventually traced several vessels from photographs of Thames river boats owned by various suspects but were never able to confirm which vessel had picked up Calvi that evening. But police did connect at least one other murder to the Calvi case. Two months after Calvi had been killed, Sergio Vaccari, an Italian drug dealer, was stabbed more than 15 times in his face, neck and chest in his flat in west London. Vaccari was later linked to hiring the boat on which Calvi was killed. He was silenced after threatening to turn informer unless some drug debts were written off.

Those involved in the murder of Roberto Calvi remain free to this day, despite the extraordinary depth of evidence provided by specialist forensic scientists.

THE YORKSHIRE RIPPER

The psychiatric side of forensic science is shrouded in mystery, but every now and again its experts astound the world of law enforcement with their abilities in the face of the most appalling crimes. Many forensic scientists – especially those who study psychological behaviour – prefer to remain in the shadows (unlike their television counterparts on shows like *Silent Witness*). As a result, relatively little is known about one such forensic expert, who played a significant role in helping to bring one of Britain's most notorious serial killers – the Yorkshire Ripper, Peter Sutcliffe – to justice.

Professor Stuart Kind helped police crack the long-unsolved case by literally plotting the murderer's path of violence. It was an unusual approach back in the early 1980s and sparked a lot of criticism at the time. It was only some years later that Professor Kind got the credit he fully deserved.

The Yorkshire Ripper police investigation itself was dogged with problematical leads, including detectives being diverted for several months by a taped message purporting to be from the murderer, in which he taunted them. Officers were convinced the voice was the actual killer, but in fact it was all a hoax and resulted in a lot of public criticism of Yorkshire Police's Ripper squad and its investigative skills.

Professor Kind originally came onto the investigation in late 1980 as a member of an advisory team which included four senior police officers. In many ways, it was a last throw of the dice by police. He was immediately treated like an eccentric, detached boffin when it came to his plans to forensically examine the case.

Kind ignored all the sceptics and eventually applied his own, unique navigational ideas in regard to the multiple murders. He reworked all the data known up to that time about the Yorkshire Ripper, who'd killed prostitutes in and around the Yorkshire city of Bradford. In the late autumn of 1980, Kind spent 17 days re-examining in minute detail the progress of the enquiry from every angle. He produced his own hypotheses of the suspect by combining a number of individual findings into a general statement, which he believed could be interpreted into being actual facts about the suspect.

Kind later explained that the mental procedure of producing such a hypothesis was extremely complex. The scientist carefully made his deductions based on the logical consequences of the information he'd been provided with.

Initially, much public criticism was aimed at Professor Kind, because he seemed – on the surface at least – to be doing the same work as the police by injecting his own version of a hunch into every aspect of his enquiries.

Professor Kind saw it as putting his own scientific hypothesis into the case. He was hoping to eventually provide many more details about the suspect that would help the investigation move forward. Professor Kind himself later conceded there was an element of non-scientific risk involved, because he was committing himself to certain information about the Yorkshire Ripper, which was not fully backed up by facts.

It eventually emerged that much of Professor Kind's knowledge about the Yorkshire Ripper was based around just one meeting with detectives leading the hunt. All his other information about the case came from newspaper reports. This strategy continued to be treated with great caution by the police and the general public. It also provoked a lot of suspicion and criticism inside the forensic science community. Some accused Professor Kind of promoting the use of outrageous guesswork, which wasn't backed up by any scientific data. He wasn't bothered. Like all good scientists, he was determined to use all the information at his disposal to come up with a winning formula. Where it came from was irrelevant if he could provide tangible results.

To all those involved in the investigation, Stuart Kind seemed like a very different kind of forensic scientist from all the others who'd worked on the Yorkshire Ripper enquiry. Also – despite being a professional forensic scientist – Professor Kind had held a relatively lowly research job for the previous four years before he joined the investigation. It was during this time that he'd mastered his own unique methods for investigating crimes. Another forensic scientist who worked on the Sutcliffe case later explained:

> Stuart came at this case from a completely different angle to everyone else. He was a stubborn character and he believed he had developed an investigative system which was very different from any other forensic expert. He chose to ignore a lot of the science and often went with his 'street' instincts. Many other scientists were far from convinced this was the best way to hunt down the Yorkshire Ripper. But, quite frankly, the police were desperate by this stage for a break in the case, they had little to lose.

Kind's first substantial move was to completely deconstruct the notion that the man the police were hunting was from outside the area where most of his victims had been killed. Many detectives were still fixated on the killer coming from the north-east of England, because that had been the accent of the male hoaxer who sent them the taunting tapes later dismissed as a fake.

Stuart Kind, on the other hand, deduced that the Ripper was a local man, because on three of the murders, investigators had found the same tyre tracks at the scene. He believed that showed the killer was just driving around looking for victims close to his own home.

The only other piece of significant evidence ever discovered by the police had been a new five-pound note, which was found in the handbag of the ripper's tenth victim, murdered on 1 October 1977, long before Kind joined the investigation. This note had been issued between Thursday 29 September and Saturday 1 October 1977 by one of two banks in the local area. The money was assumed to have been payment for sex, since five pounds in advance was the going rate for street prostitutes in the area at that time. The fact that the note had been issued in Yorkshire – where the majority of the previous Ripper cases had occurred – was considered by Professor Kind to be highly significant, because it further emphasized that the killer was local.

Then came Professor Kind's specialized navigational tests. The first one involved him establishing what he called "centre of gravity" offences. He studied a map of the area in which all 17 Yorkshire Ripper attacks had occurred and marked the location of each one with a pin. Professor Kind took an eighteenth pin and joined it to each of the 17 locations with a piece of thread. The location of that eighteenth pin – with the least amount of thread required – became the centre of gravity for all the actual offences. Kind believed the attacker came from in or around where that eighteenth pin was located, inside the city of Bradford.

Kind used a computer at the Home Office's Central Research Establishment in London to carry out a more sophisticated version of his centre of gravity exercise. This time, six separate tests were carried out. They were based on six different sets of assumptions as to which of the 17 attacks were definitely by the Ripper. The centre of gravity proved again to be in all cases near the city of Bradford, which further convinced Kind that the killer was a local man.

On 17 December 1980 – as a result of these findings by Professor Kind – a report was presented to the Chief Constable of the West Yorkshire Metropolitan Police. It recommended that a special team of detectives should be dedicated to enquiries in the Bradford area. Just a few weeks later, at 10 p.m. on Friday 2 January 1981, two police patrolmen on duty in the city of Sheffield questioned and eventually arrested Peter William Sutcliffe, who turned out to be the Yorkshire Ripper.

Sutcliffe spoke with a Bradford accent. He lived in the district of Heaton in Bradford. Heaton was halfway between Manningham and Shipley, two of the Ripper's favourite "hunting grounds" and the exact area where Stuart Kind said the killer lived after he'd carried out his unique tests.

Stuart Kind later admitted he'd first started developing his controversial forensic techniques while learning to be a navigator in the Royal Air Force during the Second World

War. He'd worked out the importance of using maps to reflect all known facts and how that often provided correct answers. The success of his work on the Yorkshire Ripper case led to a report recommending widespread changes in criminal investigations, including the broader use of computers.

On 22 May 1981, Sutcliffe was convicted of murdering 13 women and attempting to murder seven others. He was sentenced to 20 concurrent sentences of life imprisonment, which was increased to a whole life order in 2010. As a result of Professor Stuart Kind's work on the Yorkshire Ripper case, this type of non-traditional scientific analysis has since been used frequently on other cases with great success.

DENNIS NILSEN

Another of the UK's most notorious serial killers was Dennis Nilsen. He killed at least a dozen young men whom he lured back to his home in north London after plying them with alcohol in pubs in the centre of the city, during the same period Peter Sutcliffe was murdering prostitutes on the streets of Yorkshire.

But when Nilsen eventually confessed to police that he'd killed numerous young men between 1978 and 1983, he couldn't even remember their names. There were no witnesses and his victims were mainly teenage runaways, some of whose families hadn't even reported them missing in the first place.

One retired London murder squad detective explained: "Nilsen would probably have only killed two or three victims at the most if he'd committed his crimes today because of DNA and other advances in forensic science and general surveillance.

> "I'm certain we would have quickly located CCTV footage of him drinking with his victims in the bars he frequented in Central London. Then we'd have focused on getting forensic evidence from his home once we knew he was involved in those early disappearances. But back in the 1980s a killer could pick up random people to murder and then literally disappear without anyone even noticing. The only reason Nilsen was finally brought to justice was because he decided to make a full confession to the police."

In that same era, before DNA and improvements in other forensic technology, notorious American serial killers like Los Angeles' "Night Stalker" Richard Ramirez were tracked down using old-fashioned forensic work, including gathering hair comparisons, blood typing and collecting fingerprints to try and identify the offenders.

In the Night Stalker case this eventually led to a random fingerprint being found in a stolen car, which was matched to the rap sheet of 25-year-old drifter Ramirez, who'd orginally come from Texas. Back then, forensic analysts still had to painstakingly compare a suspect's fingerprints against sample cards until they found a match, because fingerprint technology was far inferior to what it is today. As recently as the early 1990s, investigators in Los Angeles were still struggling to identify murder victims if fingerprints were only partial. Today that work is done by a computer in seconds.

THE SHOREDITCH ROBBERY

Forensic investigators are not just there to investigate murders. Many of the UK's most skilled scientists have helped solve some of the biggest and most lucrative robberies of the past 60 years.

In the 1980s, most professional criminals didn't even know what the word forensic meant. They prided themselves on their use of sheer brute force and their ability to target the best robbery sites available in big cities.

The gang who pulled off Britain's biggest cash raid on a Security Express depot, in Shoreditch, east London, over the 1983 Easter bank holiday, also gave little thought to the skills of the scientists. Within minutes of getting onto the premises, they overcame the guards and wrapped them up in women's stockings and slapped a plaster over each of their mouths. With the vault doors open, the robbers transferred the cash they were after onto trolleys and sent them up on a lift to the loading bays, where they were placed in the back of a 7-ton truck. Each sack they moved along a human chain contained £100,000. After more than six hours on the premises, the gang had managed to pack bundles of bank notes in denominations of £50 downwards totalling £5,961,097 into their waiting vehicle. Their haul weighed an astonishing 5 tons.

Within days of the robbery, Scotland Yard Flying Squad officers had been given the names of the robbers by their own tame police informant. Now they needed to find proof that would stand up in a court of law. Chief robbery suspect Ronnie Knight ran nightclubs and kept his life of crime secret from his actress wife Barbara Windsor, despite his once close and open association with notorious London gangsters the Kray Twins, Ronnie and Reggie. Knight's younger brother John ran The Fox pub just around the corner from where the robbery was committed in Shoreditch.

Less than a week after the heist, Flying Squad detectives asked a forensic scientist to accompany them to John Knight's pub so they could examine the cellar, where they believed the robbery cash might have been taken immediately after the raid. The forensic expert eventually found a partial shoeprint and took samples of dust. A police photographer – who was at the scene – was recruited by the scientist to take a glass jar round various parts of the basement to take samples of the air. The cellar had a distinctive smell of damp and beer, and the forensic examiner believed that this could prove significant when it came to proving where that almost £6 million in bank notes had been hidden.

During the robber's eventual trial, jurors were taken to the same basement – to smell it. This was the first time in UK criminal history that a jury had made such a trip to the scene of an alleged crime. The jury were left in no doubt that the odour of the cash which had been recovered by that forensic scientist matched what they smelt in that basement. The forensic laboratory also matched the dust samples from the cellar to dust found on the stolen cash. This clearly proved the cash had been stored in The Fox pub, owned by Knight's brother John.

In 1985, five men including Ronnie Knight and his brother John were found guilty of robbery and handling stolen money. John Knight got 22 years and Ronnie fled to Spain but returned to Britain in 1994 and was jailed for seven years.

WITNESS FOR THE DEFENCE

The ability of forensic scientists to remain unbiased through all cases is obviously crucial to a homicide investigation. "Quite simply, we cannot take sides. We must provide the scientific evidence *not* the motivation behind a crime," one pathologist explained. "That is the job of the lawyers and the police."

One such case occurred after a deadly incident at an isolated house in the middle of the Kent countryside in January 1985. Two notorious professional criminals had met there to discuss their next move following the biggest gold bullion robbery in British criminal history.

Within a few minutes of them sitting down to talk, both men heard the homeowner's rottweilers making a commotion outside, so they went out to investigate. As one of the men passed his Ford Granada parked on the driveway, he grabbed a torch from inside it and took a knife he'd been using earlier to clean the car's battery tops. Meanwhile, two undercover police officers watching the property as part of their gold bullion robbery investigation had decided to pull out of the garden when they realized their target's three dogs were heading in their direction through the bushes.

A few moments later, the man who owned the house spotted a hooded figure dressed all in black in the foliage close to the perimeter fence of the property. The two men got into a scuffle and the criminal plunged his knife into the intruder five times in the front of his body and five times in the back. Just beyond the perimeter fence, other undercover policemen watching the property encountered the victim's partner, who'd just managed to scramble over the back wall when the house owner had appeared in the garden.

As the policeman lay bleeding, his attacker allegedly yelled at his associate: "I hope he fuckin' dies." One of the men was also alleged to have said: "Show us your ID then." Then one of the men kicked the slain undercover officer, and the same voice said: "Right, we'll blow your fucking head off." When the assailant threatened to attack the policeman again if he didn't say who he was, the officer mumbled "SAS" and passed out. His attacker later claimed he thought he'd stumbled on a rapist or a peeping Tom.

The other officer who'd scrambled to safety later recalled peering through the fence after their surveillance target had finished his assault and was standing over his victim with his wife and another known criminal close by. Moments later a police car smashed through the wrought iron gates to the house. The attacker and his wife were immediately arrested for murder and taken to a local police station. The other criminal who was present when the killing occurred was also detained.

A forensic examination of the property hours later also connected the two criminals to the stolen bullion at the centre of the original robbery investigation. They discovered globular fragments of gold on the boot mat of the Ford Granada and the other man's Vauxhall car. Police uncovered a further 11 gold bars wrapped in red-and-white cloth hidden in a shallow gully beside the garage wall. As a result, the two professional criminals were additionally charged with conspiracy to handle stolen bullion.

The killing of an undercover policeman in the grounds of that house completely overshadowed all other professional criminal activities at the time. Not only were the two criminals charged with murder but so was the wife, who was present when the knifing occurred.

Two months later – at a committal hearing at Lambeth Magistrates Court in south London – renowned forensic scientist Dr Iain West provided expert witness testimony after being called by lawyers for the wife. Her defence team wanted it to be made clear she had not taken part in the attack, despite police claims to the contrary. Iain West told the committal hearing that the 10 stabbing wounds inflicted on the undercover police officer had been so ferocious he thought it unlikely any of them could have been caused by a woman, and all the charges against the wife were dismissed.

Both gangsters appeared at the Old Bailey Criminal Court in London in November 1985. It was a case that had been dubbed "the murder trial of the decade" by the media. The original forensic scientist who attended the scene in the hours following the killing of the undercover policeman gave evidence about the ferocity of the attack and chilling details about the wounds that spelt the end of that policeman's life. The expert also stated that the police officer appeared to have been held from behind while the ferocious attack took place. However, the other criminal present on the night of the killing alleged in court that he and his underworld associate had been "fitted up" (framed) for the murder by the police and insisted they both thought the undercover officer was a burglar.

After 12 hours and 37 minutes of jury deliberation, not guilty verdicts were returned against the main criminal and the other gangster who was present at the house in Kent on that night. The jury accepted that the killing had been in self-defence, after the defendants had stumbled on the under-cover police officer hiding in the bushes of the garden.

ANGEL OF DEATH

In 1990, Professor Alec Jeffreys – founder of the DNA finger-printing system that had revolutionized worldwide crime detection a few years earlier – found himself at the centre of a bizarre case that was sparked by the recovery of the remains of a man of German origin found dead 11 years earlier in Sao Paulo, Brazil.

The skeleton was alleged to have been Josef Mengele, the notorious Nazi doctor who'd conducted experiments on Jewish prisoners during the Second World War. He was considered one of the twentieth century's most evil men.

Mengele – nicknamed the "Angel of Death" – sent about 400,000 people to the gas chambers at the Auschwitz death camp in Poland. He experimented on inmates, particularly twins, to explore chilling Nazi theories on Aryan superiority.

In 1949 – four years after the Second World War ended – Mengele arrived in South America on an International Red Cross passport under the name of an Italian national called Gregor Helmut. He'd escaped from Europe on the notorious "rat run", which enabled thousands of Nazi war criminals to flee justice. Mengele had travelled through Argentina and Paraguay and eventually settled in Brazil. His family claimed in 1979 that he'd died aged 68 in a swimming accident in the Atlantic in southern Brazil, after living in the city for 18 years. But many believed that Mengele's death never occurred and that he was still alive and hiding from authorities.

Reports of sightings of Mengele kept cropping up following his "death". There were rumours he'd faked his own death to prevent Nazi hunters from tracking him down. During the first half of the 1980s, some of these rumours gained increasing credence, and that outrage grew when more sightings of Mengele in South America were reported.

Authorities recognized that there was a need to retrieve the remains of this Nazi war criminal and establish once and for all whether they belonged to Mengele or not. In June 1985, Mengele's remains were exhumed from a grave marked "Wolfgang Gerhard" near Sao Paulo, Brazil.

Doctors initially claimed to have matched the genetic makeup of Mengele's remains with a blood sample from his son Rolf, who was said to have complied only after German officials threatened to raid another relative's grave to obtain a DNA genetic sample. But following those initial tests, there were allegations that other Nazis still on the run in South America had bribed the original forensic examiner to ensure their friend Mengele appeared to have "died", because it helped take the heat off them. As a result, these results were eventually deemed untrustworthy, and that's when it was decided to call in Professor Alec Jeffreys – already world renowned thanks to his discovery of DNA fingerprints.

Jeffreys carefully removed trace amounts of highly degraded human DNA from the shaft of the skeleton's femur. This was compared with fresh blood samples submitted by his son, Rolf, a lawyer in Freiburg, Germany. Professor Jeffreys also compared the DNA fingerprints from the remains of Mengele's first wife to make sure his son's samples were genuine. Jeffreys rapidly concluded that the remains found in Brazil belonged to Dr Mengele.

He explained to a packed press conference in 1990 how he compared the DNA recovered from Josef Mengele's femur with DNA from his son and wife. Jeffreys assured the media that the findings were 99.997 per cent conclusive. He said that nothing in science is 100 per cent certain, but that there was no room for doubt in this case. In Vienna, Simon Wiesenthal – Holocaust survivor and global Nazi hunter – said: "We now close the Mengele file. There is nothing stronger than a genetic test."

But the way Professor Jeffreys' much-coveted DNA technology had been used in this case meant that it was now having a much more far-reaching effect on a wide range of issues. He told one journalist at the time that he felt the science of DNA fingerprinting had already reached its full potential. Others would no doubt disagree.

Having in effect "created the monster" of DNA fingerprints for all sorts of very honourable and scientific reasons, Professor Alec Jeffreys realized there was a danger of it being hijacked by politicians and others with questionable agendas. His main concern was (and still is) that DNA fingerprinting raised crucial issues about balancing the use of technology to help society against an individual's right to privacy. There was no way Jeffreys could put the brakes on its development as a law enforcement tool. In any case, its benefits obviously far outweighed its disadvantages.

CHARLIE WILSON

The benefits of using forensic science to solve murders are clearly self-explanatory, but the cost of using its highly skilled technicians has inhibited the quest for justice until very recently.

No one took much notice of the pale-faced man with badly dyed, spiky blond hair sunning himself on the mini-roundabout close to an estate of detached haciendas called the Urbanización Montana, on the outskirts of Marbella, on Spain's Costa del Sol. It was June 1990. A yellow mountain bike lay beside him as he sat nonchalantly on the grass, a big, overhanging eucalyptus tree providing some shade. He stayed for hours, occasionally swigging from a bottle and rolling himself a few joints. Enjoying the sunshine. Watching and waiting.

Two hundred yards away, the spring sunshine was beating down on the immaculate lawn of the back garden of a detached whitewashed house. A gentle breeze blew in from the pine woods behind the property, causing a slight ripple on the surface of its swimming pool. In the far corner of the garden, a man in his late fifties, wearing shorts and a polo shirt, had just finished lighting a barbeque. Looking immensely pleased with himself, he crouched down to pick some thyme from a neatly trimmed bed of herbs. He was preparing a very special dinner to celebrate his thirty-fifth wedding anniversary.

Less than two miles away, another man was speaking with a hesitant voice into a payphone in a petrol station forecourt on the nearby coastal road. It was known locally as the Road of Death, having claimed the lives of many motorists and pedestrians over the years. The man slammed the phone down, got into a white van and drove onto the dual carriageway before taking the next exit and heading towards the mountains.

Back in that immaculate garden, the middle-aged man in shorts was gently whistling to himself as he sprinkled more thyme and salt onto two raw, blue steaks laid out on a plate next to the barbeque. Then he broke into Frank Sinatra's "Come Fly With Me" as if he didn't have a care in the world. The song took him back nearly 30 years, to when he and 11 others created history by pulling off the most daring train robbery in criminal history. In the sunshine of southern Spain, as his Alsatian Bo-Bo snoozed at his feet, all those memories must have seemed a million miles away. The days of professional, gentlemen criminals were long gone. Now the Costa del Sol's chilling drugs underworld was filled with trigger-happy characters settling scores with a bullet.

Nearby, the white van had reached the mini-roundabout where the man with the yellow mountain bike waited under the shade of that big eucalyptus tree. He nodded briefly at the van driver, who parked his vehicle just beyond the roundabout and got out. Separately, they walked up a quiet side street dotted with ornate streetlamps and houses on one side, faced by a huge plot of land. They passed number 7, a white house, followed by numbers 9 and 11. Instead of a number on the next house there was the name "Chequers". They'd been here before, so they knew it was the one they wanted. Bougainvillea and carefully cultivated shrubbery covered much of the front of the property.

The middle-aged man was still in the back garden when the doorbell rang. Bo-Bo barked briefly but settled down as soon as his master told him to. The owner's wife answered the door to find the pale-faced man standing on the doorstep in a grey tracksuit, a baseball cap pulled low on his forehead. His yellow mountain bike was leaning against a wall. With a distinct south London accent, he asked the woman, "Is he in?" She nodded and told him to put his bike in the porch in case someone tried to steal it.

Moments later, the wife called to say he had a visitor. He put down a knife he'd been using to cut tomatoes and cucumbers for a salad and greeted the young man with a grimace and nodded towards the patio area next to the pool. His dog Bo-Bo curled up in a shady corner of the garden. As the two men walked across the patio, the homeowner's wife heard raised voices but decided to stay in the house while they talked business.

Minutes later, the visitor suddenly karate-kicked the older man in the testicles. He doubled over, struggling for breath. His nose was broken by a crunching karate chop. Bo-Bo, leaping to his master's aid, received a vicious kick in the chest that snapped his front leg and shoulder bone like a twig. The assailant produced a gleaming silver Smith & Wesson 9 mm pistol from under his tracksuit top and fired at point-blank range. The first bullet pierced the carotid artery of the older man's neck. The second entered his mouth and exited from the back of his head.

In the kitchen, his wife noticed two loud bangs. At first, she thought they'd come from a building site behind the house. Then she heard Bo-Bo screeching and rushed to the garden to see the faithful dog wounded on the ground while her husband staggered towards the pool, blood spurting from his neck. She later said, "There was blood, blood, blood everywhere. He was desperately trying to stand up. He stared at me, but could not talk." Her husband held his finger to his open mouth. Blood was streaming from it. He tried to point to the back wall, over which the gunman had escaped. The shooter could easily have waited and turned his gun on his target's wife.

Contract killings on Spain's notorious Costa del Crime were two a penny. But this was the cold-blooded murder of former Great Train Robber Charlie Wilson, who thought he could handle the deadliest underworld of all.

Spain in the early 1990s was a very different place from the UK when it came to forensic investigations of murders. Local police and forensic scientists were equally badly paid, and the death of a gangster at the hands of another criminal simply didn't merit a proper post-mortem examination. As one recently retired Marbella police detective later told me: "The local police force was broke back in those days. We didn't even have any computers and when one criminal was killed by another it was considered unimportant. Post mortems were only undertaken when it involved murders of innocent people. We all saw the bullet wounds in Wilson's body so why bother wasting our money on a pathologist cutting him up?" Instead, the corpse of Charlie Wilson remained in the morgue of the local hospital for a few days before being released to the family for burial in London.

Some time after Wilson's murder, I met up with one of the detectives leading the supposed "hunt" for Wilson's killer and requested to see the file on the case. We were in a small, bare office on the first floor of the old Marbella police station at the time. It was a shabby, overcrowded two-storey building tucked away a dozen blocks behind the sandy beaches and garish beach bars frequented by so many holidaymakers. The detective opened an old-fashioned filing cabinet and joked about how they still didn't have computers in their office because they were too expensive. He handed me the yellowing file that had Charlie Wilson's name on it.

I opened it expecting to find some kind of coroner's report and lots of material about the scene of the crime. Instead there was just one page and on it was written one sentence in Spanish. "*Asesinada por otra criminal.*" Roughly translated into English that means: "Killed by another criminal." The detective smiled as I looked up at him and shrugged his shoulders. When I asked about a pathologist's examination he laughed even louder. "That's it, señor. We don't waste our money finding out what we already know."

I'm told forensic investigation has come on in leaps and bounds in Spain in more recent years, but none of that was going to help track down the professional assassin who gunned down Charlie Wilson. His killer has never been apprehended. When I contacted Malaga police for an update on whether a cold case investigation might be launched one day, I was told it was not a priority and was unlikely to ever happen. As one renowned UK forensic scientist said at the time: "The murder of Wilson is important in the story of forensic science because it shows just why proper pathology procedures are carried out these days, even in places like southern Spain. The saddest thing about this case is that his killer will never be caught because the police at the time didn't think it was worth paying for a forensic investigation. I heard the police didn't even bother collecting any significant evidence from the scene of the crime."

But it was a very different story a few months later when the Spanish police authorities knew that the eyes of the world were upon them after an even more notorious man died on their territory.

ROBERT MAXWELL

High-profile deaths can often lead to additional pressure being piled on forensic scientists to come up with conclusions that suit all the relevant parties. This can threaten to distort the truth in certain instances. "Forensic scientists just want to get on with their examinations. They don't like being dragged into the limelight of high-profile cases if they can help it," commented one recently retired UK pathologist.

And none came bigger than London publisher Robert Maxwell. On 5 November 1991, he either fell, jumped or was pushed overboard from his yacht *Lady Ghislaine* as it was moored off the Canary island of Tenerife. I'd worked for 22-stone Maxwell on his newspaper the *Daily Mirror* in the mid-1980s and dealt with him personally many times. He was not the most pleasant of characters. And by the autumn of 1991, he was being chased for debts that amounted to tens of millions of pounds, and his business empire was crumbling. So when I heard that this obese former Czech immigrant and alleged war hero had toppled off the back of his beloved yacht after he'd moaned at the captain about the air-conditioning, I can't say I was particularly upset or surprised.

143

Less than half an hour after his disappearance, a fisherman reported spotting a large body floating on its back in the sea, a few miles from where Maxwell's yacht had been cruising. Not long after that sighting, a Spanish helicopter was hovering above the remains of one of Britain's most notorious business magnates and reported back by radio. "Naked, stiff and floating."

Apart from his uncharacteristic isolation on board his yacht during that last voyage, there is no clue as to what was really going on in one-time war hero Maxwell's mind at the time of his death. Yes, he'd shamelessly plundered his own company's pension fund to prop up his precarious finances. He was facing intolerable pressure. And yet, as Tom Bower, his biographer, pointed out in *Maxwell: The Final Verdict*, this was not new: "Anyone who had fought on the front line from the Normandy beaches to Germany, facing constant danger and death for months on end from the enemy's snipers and shells, was unlikely to suffer fear. And he had overcome much worse."

That is not to say Maxwell wasn't concerned about his personal safety. The *Lady Ghislaine* had security cameras at key points and the crew were under orders to keep watch on the gangplank when in port, in case anyone tried to board the boat. At night, the radar scanned for any vessels approaching. If Maxwell had been murdered, the assassin or assassins would have had to get aboard, force him into the sea and escape – all without anyone hearing or seeing them.

After Maxwell's body was recovered, the crew of his yacht were interviewed by an examining magistrate in Tenerife, who found nothing suspicious. There were no apparent puncture marks on his body, either. There was some slight bruising, but nothing to indicate an assault. It has since been alleged that on the night he died, Maxwell fell forward over a low rail and ended up dangling for some time over the water 10 ft below. He clung on with his weaker left arm, tearing the muscles on that side of his body. Some are convinced that Maxwell remained alive in the water and shouted and waved but that the crew heard and saw nothing. What we can say for certain is that he was 68, was in poor health, weighed a vast amount and had a weak heart and lungs.

The first autopsy on Maxwell's body was carried out in Tenerife. It found no seawater in his lungs, which would have indicated drowning. Instead, the local pathologist – Dr Carlos Lopez de Lamela – concluded the publishing magnate had died of a heart attack.

Two days later, another examination was held in Israel, where Maxwell's body had been flown for burial so he could be given a hero's internment in Mount Sinai, after apparently spending many years as an unofficial spy for the Israelis. This time a Dr Yehuda Hiss was in charge. Also present was London pathologist Dr Iain West, whom I'd first met 15 years earlier. He had been hired by an insurance company due to make a £20 million payment out to the Maxwell family, depending on whether his death was accidental, a suicide or murder.

Both men saw clear evidence of badly ripped muscles and some internal bleeding and apparent signs that Maxwell might have put up a struggle before plunging into the water. But West and Hiss could not examine Maxwell's heart, because it was still in the laboratory back in Tenerife. Despite this, Dr Hiss still managed to conclude that Maxwell had suffered a heart attack and drowned. He later said he could see the telltale signs in the body, without needing to examine the organ itself. Dr West disagreed: he said there was no heart attack, but that Maxwell had simply fallen into the sea and drowned, which might mean he committed suicide.

By all accounts these examinations by three respected forensic scientists were seen as highly controversial, no doubt partly because each of them felt their knowledge and skill was being questioned by the involvement of the other two. Three pathologists, three different verdicts, one body. The official ruling at a Madrid inquest decided a month later that death was caused by heart problems, combined with accidental drowning. Murder was ruled out by the Spanish judge, but many remained convinced he'd committed suicide.

Spanish coroner Dr Lopez later explained: "We are saying that he probably died of ischemic heart disease." This was described as a condition in which not enough oxygen-rich blood reached the heart. Dr Lopez said detailed studies performed in Madrid had found no proof of an actual heart attack but the disease itself had killed him, which was as good as saying he'd died of a heart attack. Dr Lopez insisted there was no evidence of poison, alcohol or significant doses of medicines. "We cannot confirm absolutely whether he was alive or dead when he fell into the sea," Dr Lopez told journalists. "That is the most difficult point." But Dr Lopez added: "He did not have the classic signs of drowning."

The mystery of what had really happened to Robert Maxwell was being tainted by huge doses of colourful speculation, sparked by the big man's notoriety. However, all three experts agreed on one point: Maxwell's body had no telltale signs of someone who'd been in the sea for a long time. His skin was not shrivelled from the exposure to seawater and he was not sunburnt.

Then came allegations that Maxwell had come into possession of tapes proving British security service MI6's involvement in the murder of the Bulgarian dissident writer Georgi Markov and that British security agents had killed him to ensure he kept silent. But this seems very far-fetched, and some believe this was deliberate misinformation aired in public to divert attention away from the real reason Maxwell died. Others claimed that Maxwell was fearful that his activities on behalf of Israeli security service Mossad were about to be exposed, so Mossad had him assassinated to stop him from talking about them.

The captain of Maxwell's yacht later claimed Maxwell's cabin door was locked from the outside – so how had he planned to get back in? Surely, if he had just stepped out for some air or to urinate over the side – which he often did – he would not have bothered to lock the door.

Most people who intend to kill themselves tend to do so fully clothed. He was naked. Another question was why did he cause himself agonizing pain by clinging onto the side and shredding his muscles? Did he have second thoughts?

Other indications emerged that seemed to back up claims that he did not take his own life. There was no note. The night his body was found, his cabin was cleaned and tidied by the crew, so that his wife Betty could use it. If there had been any clues lying around, they 'd been swept away. That seemed very convenient. Maxwell's wife Betty was adamant that her husband would never have committed suicide. She believed from the outset that it was death by natural causes.

In the UK, the Spanish autopsy results were attacked by respected veteran forensic pathologist Dr Bernard Knight. He was by this time the president of the British Association in Forensic Medicine. He said: "There is still no objective evidence of what happened. What we have here is a man with a heart disease and a lung disease found in the sea. The fact that he has these diseases does not mean he died from any of them." He added: "They can't prove he drowned; they can't prove he didn't drown. They can't prove a heart attack; they can't prove there wasn't a heart attack. So they are assuming. We would call this unascertained death."

Dr Knight even publicly labelled Spanish forensic medicine as backward. "Spain has the worst system of forensic medicine in Europe," Dr Knight told journalists at the time. Judging from what I'd witnessed following the murder of Great Train Robber Charlie Wilson in southern Spain only a few months earlier, Dr Knight may have had a point. Dr Lopez hit back by revealing that he'd had access to the results of medical check-ups on Maxwell made in a hospital in Nancy, France over the previous decade. These clearly showed that his oxygen intake was progressively diminishing. "It was well below average in 1988, so it must have been even more serious now," said Dr Lopez. This once again implied natural causes were the most likely cause of death.

Outspoken British forensic scientist Dr Iain West, meanwhile, continued to declare that Maxwell's death was likely to be suicide. A claims underwriter for Robert Maxwell's life insurance policy said Dr West had not told him that anything suggesting violence was involved in the death. "As far as I'm aware, he saw no signs of any violence or any problem," said a spokesman for the insurance company. But Iain West knew only too well that if he had concluded that Maxwell had been killed, the insurers would have refused to pay the beneficiaries of the policy, which were Maxwell companies.

* * *

Some time after the dust seemed to have settled on the story of Maxwell's death, there was a final twist; still photos emerged which had been taken from a videotape recording of the forensic examination conducted on Maxwell's remains at Abu Kabir Forensic Institute in Tel Aviv on the night of 9–10 November. This was the autopsy jointly overseen by Dr Iain West and Israeli Dr Hiss.

Paris Match magazine – who published the photos – claimed the examination found several bruises on Maxwell's face, shoulders, stomach and calves, indicating he was beaten before he fell – or was thrown – from his yacht. The magazine quoted the forensic scientists from the videotape describing the bruising on Maxwell's body. "We showed the pictures to French experts," said *Paris Match*. "The experts were explicit: the multiple bruises on the body of the ex-press magnate indicated he was attacked before his death." Loic Le Ribault – a French police forensic specialist – was quoted by the magazine saying that "according to the photos, it is highly probable that the victim was hit in the back of the head with a blunt instrument". Another expert quoted by the magazine stated that the injuries alone probably did not cause death.

Speculation about how Maxwell died has continued to this day. Was it suicide, heart failure, an accident of fate or murder? Not even some of the finest forensic minds in the world could come up with a final verdict on how he died. As one of Maxwell's former employees on his newspaper the *Daily Mirror* later told me: "Bob would have loved all the attention his death attracted because he was a great showman and he'd even have had a chuckle that not even the scientists could get to the bottom of what happened to him."

THE RANGE ROVER KILLINGS

Preserving a crime scene is of paramount importance to forensic scientists, as has already been clearly outlined in this book. But occasionally, the breakthrough evidence that investigators expect to be forthcoming is nowhere to be found – and that can sometimes lead to questionable convictions.

In December 1996, a Range Rover was discovered parked down an isolated farm track in the Essex countryside by two passing farmers in the early hours of the morning. Two bodies were slumped in the front of the vehicle and another one in the nearside back. One of the windows had been shot out from the outside.

Within hours, forensic scientists and police officers were meticulously combing the track and surrounding area for any clues. Overhead, a helicopter swept over nearby fields with a heat-seeking camera looking for any other evidence of what had happened. Police believed notorious Essex criminals Craig Rolfe, Pat Tate and Tony Tucker had been lured to their deaths by the promise of a massive drug deal.

Having completed their on-the-ground examination, forensic scientists arranged for a transport lorry to carefully lift the entire vehicle with the three corpses still inside onto the truck's flatbed. This meant the bodies would remain untouched inside the Range Rover exactly as they'd died during the mass shooting near the country village of Rettendon. The transport lorry was driven under a police escort one hundred miles north to Leicester University's prestigious forensic laboratory, whose renowned facilities feature regularly in so many of the cases covered in this book.

Over the following days, the Range Rover, complete with the victims, was minutely examined, before the bodies of the three criminals were finally removed and given individual post-mortems. Clearly, gangsters Craig Rolfe, Tony Tucker and Pat Tate had all been targeted from close range. All three had been shot a total of eight times. Forensic examiners were able to ascertain that Tate had had time to put up his hands and hunch down while Tucker and Rolfe had been killed instantly. After what appeared to be two killers reloaded, one of the two shooters appeared to have taken the gun from his associate and shot each of the men behind their ears just to make sure they were dead. Forensics could tell this from the different type of bullets used on those fatal final shots.

But despite having this intact death scene, forensic investigators failed to find any significant clues as to who actually carried out the triple murder. They even struggled to ascertain the exact time that the three men had been shot. One veteran forensic scientist explained: "That Range Rover should have been the perfect crime scene in a sense, but even with the vehicle parked in a secure location for forensic examination, scientists couldn't find any really significant clues which might help the police to identify the killers."

The case went ominously quiet after that, until a police informant stepped forward and told detectives that he had driven the killers to and from the murder scene. With this vital witness, it seemed that the lack of hard forensic evidence was no longer so crucial to the case. More than two years later, two men, Jack Whomes, 36, from Suffolk and Michael Steele, 55, from Bentley, in Essex, were found guilty of the gangland triple murder and received three life sentences with a minimum of 15 years.

It was not until 2003 – more than five years later – that new Cell Site Analysis evidence would put in question the prosecution of one of the alleged hitmen. CSA is the science of reconstructing the physical movements of a mobile telephone or telecommunication device. This can result in crucial evidence when it comes to contact between individuals, including their proximity to the scene of a crime as well as the patterns of movement of any suspects, which can test the ability of alibi evidence. CSA can include radio frequency and what is known as Call Mapping. This is often a crucial process within Cell Site Analysis investigations, because it exposes the operational footprint of individuals and groups through telecommunication masts, cell sites and radio signal antennae.

A cell site specialist uncovered "significant" evidence that seemed to discount the involvement of one of the convicted killers from the scene of the now notorious gangland triple murder. Mechanic Jack Whomes had earlier been placed at the scene of the crime through mobile phone records as well as supposedly "questionable" evidence from that alleged gangland informant, who claimed that he acted as the getaway driver for Whomes and his fellow hitman Steele. The key forensic evidence at the original trial had centred on two phone calls allegedly made by Whomes, which were picked up on two different cell phone masts, just after the shootings. But this new cell site expert established that one of the transmitters that picked up the call – at a place called Ingatestone – was not within range at the scene, which suggested alleged killer Whomes was not at the scene after all.

Further independent forensic tests on Whomes' phone exposed more far-reaching reliability questions about the original mobile phone evidence. The new investigator made dozens of calls at various places and heights up and down the lane where the murders occurred. But not one of those calls was routed through the second cell site, at Hockley, which the prosecution at the original triple murder trial had said was within range. This clearly further implied that Whomes was elsewhere at the time of the actual killings.

This was one of the first cases in the United Kingdom to use CSA to reconstruct the movement of a mobile telephone handset. As a result of these cell site findings, the Criminal Cases Review Commission launched a re-examination of Whomes' case. At the time of writing, they had yet to make a final announcement on the appeal against his conviction.

DR DAVID KELLY

All forensic experts rightly consider themselves scientists first and foremost and investigators second. Many of them argue that they are there to find evidence that proves the truth. The rest is down to the police, lawyers, juries and judges. However, sometimes the significance of a public event can overwhelm and undermine an expert's evidence and unfairly call into question the abilities of that professional scientist.

This occurred in 2003 when UK weapons expert Dr David Kelly was identified in newspapers as the man then prime minister Tony Blair's Labour government believed was the source of a highly controversial BBC report on Iraq. Kelly was well used to talking to journalists behind the scenes, but now he found himself at the centre of a row between the government and the BBC after well-publicized claims that Downing Street had "sexed up" a dossier on Iraq's weapons capability.

Following Dr Kelly's public exposure by the BBC as a secret source for the UK media, he gave evidence to British members of parliament in which he insisted he was not the main informant behind the story. But two days after his testimony, 59-year-old Dr Kelly was found dead in dense woodland a few miles from his Oxfordshire home after apparently taking his own life. Not surprisingly, his family were traumatized.

Pathologist Dr Nicholas Hunt attended the scene where Dr Kelly's body was discovered. He eventually found a series of wounds on Dr Kelly's left wrist which had "completely severed" the ulnar artery. He estimated David Kelly's time of death as being between 4.15 p.m. on 17 July and 1.15 a.m. on 18 July.

After a post-mortem, Dr Hunt reported: "The orientation and arrangement of the wounds over the left wrist are typical of self-inflicted injury." He added: "There is no positive pathological evidence to indicate that this man has been subjected to a sustained, violent assault prior to his death. There is no evidence from the post-mortem or my observations at the scene to indicate that the deceased had been dragged or otherwise transported to the location at which his body was found." Dr Hunt emphasized that, while the wrist wounds were the main cause of death, an excessive amount of painkillers Dr Kelly had taken, plus "apparently clinically silent coronary artery disease" had both played a part in "bringing about death more certainly and more rapidly than would have otherwise been the case".

But Dr Kelly's role and subsequent actions as an alleged informant for journalists during the Iraq weapons scandal left many wondering if he'd been silenced by his critics rather than having committed suicide. So began a sustained campaign by a group of British scientists, who believed that the suicide verdict was "unsafe".

One of those experts – radiologist Stephen Frost – told reporters at the time that it would be "shameful if the truth about the suspicious death" was suppressed in a similar way to that in which details about the footballing tragedy that left 96 Liverpool FC fans dead had been. Other members of the same group, including scientists Andrew Watt, David Halpin and Christopher Burns-Cox, insisted that the investigation into Dr Kelly's death had been inadequate and had failed to examine a number of questions over the circumstances surrounding the discovery of Dr Kelly's body. They insisted there was insufficient evidence to prove beyond reasonable doubt that Dr Kelly had killed himself.

These experts claimed that Dr Kelly's wrist wounds were not likely to have been life-threatening, making the official cause of death – a haemorrhage – "extremely unlikely". Questions were asked as to why no fingerprints had been found on the knife that he had apparently used to slit his wrists, and as to how Dr Kelly had obtained a packet of co-proxamol painkillers, remnants of which were found in his blood stream. The British scientists wanted to know why Dr

Kelly's blood and stomach contained only a non-toxic dose of the drug. There were concerns as to why Dr Kelly's body was not first spotted by a police helicopter with thermal imaging cameras, which flew over the wood where his corpse was eventually found – a long time later – in the hours after he first went missing.

It seemed that the furore surrounding Dr Kelly's death would not go away. Even the original pathologist Dr Hunt called for more openness and said he would welcome an inquest, adding: "I've nothing to hide." Dr Hunt was particularly upset by the claim that there was not enough blood at the scene to support the theory that Dr Kelly died after slashing his own wrist. He later explained: "In actual fact there were big, thick clots of blood inside the sleeve, which came down over the wrist, and a lot of blood soaked into the ground."

Dr Hunt even spoke publicly about his own feelings about the case. He said: "I felt very, very sorry for David Kelly and the way he had been treated by the government. I had every reason to look for something untoward and would dearly love to have found something. It was an absolute classic case of self-inflicted injury. You could illustrate a textbook with it." The pathologist added that there was "nothing to suggest" the body had been moved, another claim from critics of the investigation.

Following Dr Kelly's suicide, British Prime Minister Tony Blair set up a government enquiry under Lord Hutton, a former Lord Chief Justice of Northern Ireland. That enquiry eventually concluded that Kelly had committed suicide and that no other parties had been involved in Kelly's death.

Unusually, an inquest opened into Dr Kelly's death was never completed. The debate over Kelly's death continued for at least the next seven or eight years. The case was reviewed between 2010 and 2011 by the UK government's Attorney General Dominic Grieve, and he concluded that there was "overwhelmingly strong" evidence that Kelly had committed suicide.

Some of those forensic scientists who'd originally questioned the suicide verdict later issued a public statement that Kelly's death "may represent one of the gravest miscarriages of justice to occur in this country". As one UK forensic scientist later pointed out: "I completely appreciate the suspicions aired over Dr Kelly's death but if some of the country's most esteemed forensic experts can't find concrete evidence that he was killed as opposed to committing suicide then this case deserves to be closed."

DIANE CHENERY-WICKENS

Improvements in forensic investigation techniques over the previous two decades meant that by 2008 scientists were at the forefront of helping to solve most serious crimes in the UK. At this time, the government-run Forensic Science Service handled most important cases. And one particularly significant murder enquiry won the FSS multiple plaudits across the world of law enforcement.

On the afternoon of 24 January 2008, Emmy award-winning make-up artist Diane Chenery-Wickens was supposed to have joined her husband David in London after a meeting at the BBC in the west of the city. But she never turned up. Her husband telephoned the police to report her missing before returning to their home at Hazelden Cottage, in Duddleswell, near Uckfield, in East Sussex.

Mr Chenery-Wickens – a 52-year-old psychic healer – was eventually interviewed by police, and immediately professed his innocence of any involvement in his wife's disappearance, even before detectives had asked him any questions. Detectives soon became convinced he was lying, and police search teams dressed in white-and-blue protective suits were drafted in to comb the woods around the Chenery-Wickens' isolated house to hunt for clues.

At the same time, items from the couple's house and car were bagged, taped, sealed and sent to one of the FSS's laboratories, located in a grim concrete bunker in a south London suburb, on the site of what was once an abattoir. On arrival at the laboratory, everything was carefully recorded on the main computer and filing system before being transferred to a central store unit where an inventory was kept, so there was a record of anyone handling the items. But missing from the first batch sent by investigators to the FSS were Diane Chenery-Wickens' watch and rings. They'd not been found by police at the cottage.

Over the following few weeks, forensic scientists led by Dr Sarah Jacob and her team began the painstaking process of going through all the items. Forensic scientists examined thirteen pairs of shoes, along with images of another eight pairs, to try and match them with a partial footprint found in the couple's Audi A4. The shoes were targeted by the FSS because of the laboratory they now ran, which contained the most comprehensive database of footwear patterns in the UK. It included sole and upper shoe images and brand logos and even highlighted specific examples of each type of footwear.

This database was essential in order to link the correct type of shoe with that single print in the car, even though it was nothing more than an imprint. The plan had been to quickly identify that footwear mark, which would in turn lead investigators to the killer. But despite all this technical expertise, no matches were found, and while forensic specialists continued their examination of all the items taken from the Chenery-Wickens home, the police investigation itself was starting to flounder.

A few weeks later, police were called to a wood near the Chenery-Wickens cottage after a dog walker reported a strong smell. Forensics from FSS were dispatched to the scene and tentatively uncovered skeletal remains just beneath the surface of the earth.

The body was that of Diana Chenery-Wickens. That in itself proved little. Forensics needed to uncover direct forensic and evidential links to her husband or whoever else might have been responsible for her death. A further police search of the Chenery-Wickens cottage followed, and Diane's wedding and eternity rings were found. Her close friends had insisted to police that Diane wore them constantly, so police suspected that the items had been removed from her body and placed back in the cottage.

Detectives delivered the two rings to DNA specialists at the FSS's laboratory in Lambeth. Other items belonging to Diana Chenery-Wickens and her husband remained at another FSS laboratory in the suburbs of south London to avoid any risk of cross-contamination. The wedding and eternity rings were examined with an illuminated microscope to see if there was any staining that resembled blood. Miniscule specks on both rings gave a positive chemical test result, which confirmed they were blood.

But FSS scientists not only proved that victim Diana's blood was on both rings, but that they'd been removed while she was actually still bleeding and alive. This was a significant breakthrough for the investigation, because both items had not been recovered when the Chenery-Wickens cottage had been originally searched shortly after Diana's disappearance. At David Chenery-Wickens' eventual murder trial, prosecutors told the court he'd revisited his wife's body at her burial site in the woods and removed the jewellery to prevent her being identified. That jewellery had been splattered with blood during the original attack on Diana. Without that forensic evidence, David Chenery-Wickens would not have been convicted of murder at Lewes Crown Court in March 2009 and jailed for life with a minimum tariff of 18 years.

JO YEATES

By 2010, forensic scientists had long since fully mastered the skill of enhancing weak and miniscule samples of DNA and then retrieving them from crime scenes. As a result, forensic experts were in demand to work on missing persons cases to try and establish why someone had disappeared and where they might be.

Jo Yeates, 25, was a landscape architect who'd only recently moved to Bristol, in the west of England, after the company she and her boyfriend Greg Reardon both worked for relocated from Winchester, in Hampshire, early in 2010. In October 2010, the young couple moved into a downstairs flat at Canynge Road in Clifton, on the edge of the city. As Christmas approached, the couple organized a party for friends at their flat.

Greg went off to Sheffield in his native Yorkshire to visit his family for the weekend before Christmas Day. Jo told work colleagues she was not looking forward to missing him for a whole weekend – their first time apart since they'd moved to Bristol. With her boyfriend having already left for the night, Jo Yeates went for an after-work drink with friends at a pub called the Bristol Ram in Park Street, Bristol. Afterwards, she headed home to the flat. En route, Jo purchased a pizza and a couple of bottles of cider at three shops. She reached home sometime around 8.30 p.m. but was never seen again.

When boyfriend Greg returned from Sheffield on the Sunday night, he found the couple's cat hadn't been fed and Jo was nowhere to be seen. Chillingly, when he called her phone again, he heard it ring in the pocket of her coat, hanging up in the hall.

That Sunday night, and over the following Monday and Tuesday, police began investigating Jo's disappearance.

Meanwhile, her many friends swung into action with social media appeals as well. Joanna's father David, mother Theresa, brother Chris and boyfriend Greg all appeared at an emotional press conference appeal on the Tuesday after she'd gone missing. A report in the following day's local paper quoted Jo's father addressing his daughter directly: "Whatever the reason that you have not been in touch over the last few days, we want you to know that we love you dearly," he said.

Hours after this, the police contacted one of the UK's new privately run forensic laboratories, LGC, about their unique "call out" service. One of LGC's body fluids and DNA specialists was brought in to try and help ascertain what had happened to Jo. The forensic team began by examining items collected from Joanna's home. They were expressly looking for all traces of DNA belonging to other individuals. Samples were taken, but they would mean little unless there was someone out there who matched them.

On Christmas Day 2010, with snow lying deep on the ground, the frozen body of Jo Yeates was discovered dumped on the side of the road near the entrance to a quarry in Failand, on the other side of the Avon Gorge from Clifton, some three miles from Jo's home in Bristol. After the body was found, the fire service had to be called in by police to activate a winch mechanism in order to lift it out for removal to a morgue, because it was frozen solid.

FGC forensic examiners attended the scene to supervise the removal of the victim's clothing and to ensure that any body fluids were preserved. Forty-eight hours of intense groundwork followed, during which the victim and her clothing were all examined so that reports could be sent to detectives hunting for Jo's killers. The forensics took samples from the victim's breasts and three areas of her jeans.

The initial tests on Jo Yeates' body by forensic pathologist Dr Russell Delaney were hampered because it was still frozen when it arrived at the laboratory. The sub-zero temperatures made it far harder for forensic experts to obtain potentially vital evidence. It took two days for the cause of death – strangulation – to be established. Some police officers feared that the appalling weather conditions which affected Bristol around the time of Jo's death might actually help her killer or killers escape justice.

Dr Delaney eventually established through a post-mortem that Jo had suffered at least 43 injuries during the struggle that ended her life. The pathologist also found red bruise marks on her neck and chin, and blood underneath her nose. He had no doubt these injuries were sustained while she was still alive. Delaney deduced through the condition of Jo's body that she'd been on that roadside for "several days" of extremely cold weather and that this had led to her remains being literally embedded in the snow. The police had initially thought Jo's body had been dumped at the roadside only a few hours before being found by walkers.

Avon and Somerset Police were warned by pathologist Dr Delaney that further forensic tests could still take "weeks and weeks" to carry out. There was one positive aspect to the bad weather, though. Important chemical evidence had been well-preserved for analysis thanks to the frozen state of the body.

Jo's murder shook Bristol and the whole of Britain. It would eventually leave four families broken forever, and its impact is still felt today.

Those early days following the discovery of Jo's body were frustrating for forensic scientists and police alike. Many of them were well aware that the public had come to expect such cases to be solved very quickly, just as they'd seen in episodes of TV series like *Silent Witness*. Eventually, police publicly announced in an emotional press conference what they believed had happened to Jo. They revealed there had been no forced entry into Jo's flat. Her coat, phone and keys were found there. Police said they were working on the correct assumption that she'd been killed in her flat and her body removed and dumped on that roadside.

Police attention then turned to Jo's neighbours. One neighbour called Vincent Tabak even called police from his Christmas break back home in Holland when he heard they were speaking to everyone who was in the vicinity at the time of Jo's death. During his phone call to police, Tabak said he thought his landlord Christopher Jeffreys had moved his car that night.

Schoolmaster Christopher Jeffreys – who lived upstairs – was arrested, held and questioned, on the day before New Year's Eve.

But Mr Jeffreys was a small man aged 65, as his legal team repeatedly pointed out during the maximum 96 hours he was allowed to be held by police. That meant it was unlikely he'd have even been able to overpower a physically fit young woman like Jo Yeates, let alone strangle her with his bare hands. So while Mr Jeffreys was being questioned in custody by detectives in Bristol, a detective constable called Karen Thomas was sent to Holland to meet that other neighbour, Vincent Tabak, to try and build the case against Mr Jeffreys.

Soon after meeting Tabak, DC Thomas sensed that something wasn't quite right about this softly spoken Dutchman. Tabak provided his statement, but then asked the detective a lot of questions, specifically about the forensic work on the case. DC Thomas travelled back from Holland highly suspicious about Vincent Tabak.

Back in Bristol, Mr Jeffreys was released. He suffered the additional blow of having to read what amounted to a character assassination of him in the national press, printed while he was in custody. It was only after this that police turned their attention fully to 32-year-old Dutchman Vincent Tabak, who'd now returned from his holiday in Holland completely unaware that detectives were looking closely at him as a likely murder suspect.

Two days later, police arrested Tabak. After taking samples of DNA from the 6-foot Dutchman, it was established that Tabak had left traces of his own DNA on Jo's body when he carried her from her flat to his car. Detectives also discovered that Tabak had a dark, secret obsession with violent pornography.

Initially, forensic scientists came up with DNA samples that matched Vincent Tabak, but those samples were of poor quality due to the high salt levels where the body had been found following that heavy snowfall. As a result, the LGC forensic team had to use a newly developed technique which purified, concentrated and enhanced what had seemed to be unusable DNA. Samples were taken with a cotton swab which was allowed to dry completely before being frozen. After that, a laser was used to target the tiny DNA cells collected on that swab. This provided the all-important DNA data to forensic examiners.

In the end, it was impossible to say where that DNA specifically came from, but forensic scientists from LGC assured detectives that the probability of it not being a match with Tabak was less than one in a billion. And as is so often the case with DNA evidence, once this was presented to Tabak he confessed to murdering Jo Yeates, so any question marks concerning the DNA evidence were no longer relevant. One prominent UK forensic scientist later explained:

In a perfect world, DNA evidence is the breakthrough which forces a criminal to confess to his crime before he gets to court. The problem is that if a prosecution relies entirely on DNA evidence, it leaves the forensic expert open to all sorts of pressure if he or she appears in court as a witness. Defence lawyers often accuse us of being biased or in the pay of the police. All you can do is tell the truth and not exaggerate anything.

If something isn't cut and dried you must say that, even if it leaves a measure of doubt on the guilt of a defendant. It's not our job to prosecute criminals.

The subsequent court case later heard that soon after Jo arrived home on the day of her murder, Vincent Tabak knocked on the door and entered her flat. It was the first time they'd met. He'd lived in the neighbouring flat for 18 months, but Jo and Greg were recent arrivals and hadn't bumped into the Dutchman and his girlfriend yet.

Why Tabak actually murdered Jo is unknown. He claimed in court that he had "accidentally killed her" while trying to stifle her yells for help. Jo's screams as Tabak attacked her were heard by a woman attending a nearby party that night, and another neighbour. But they had no idea where they came from.

Having strangled Jo in her own flat, Tabak carried her body out under the cover of darkness before dumping her in the snow on the side of that road.

At the end of October 2011, Vincent Tabak was found guilty of the murder of Joanna Yeates. He was jailed for life, with a minimum term of 20 years.

THE HATTON GARDEN GANG

Many old-school professional criminals in the UK have been forced into early retirement because they recognize they're out of their depth when it comes to new technology, especially the latest developments in forensic science. As a former bank robber called Lenny once told me: "There used to be this aura of invincibility around villains like us. We was considered untouchable back in the good old days when we robbed banks and held up security vans. Mind you, there was no DNA, computers or even mobile fuckin' phones then."

Ultimate proof that forensic science has turned the tables on such veteran criminals occurred in April 2015, when a gang of old age pensioners broke into a safety deposit vault in Hatton Garden, central London. The total stolen was said to have a value exceeding £200 million. The raid was dubbed "the Hatton Garden Job", and it turned out to be the largest burglary in British criminal history.

But within days of the actual break-in, police officers and forensic experts had methodically recovered, recorded and packaged more than four hundred pieces of potential evidence, which were then profiled for DNA, fingerprints and other forensic tests. Specialist police photographers mapped out the crime scene with tape using hi-tech digital cameras to film every inch of the inside of the premises. The police and forensic experts refused, for three days following the raid, to allow anyone into the vault while they continued their detailed examination of it.

The old-age raiders had left rubbish all over the basement area, and the wrought-iron cage door into the vault had been smashed in half. There were an angle grinder, concrete drills and crowbars found amid battered security boxes strewn across the ground of the vault. It was all invaluable evidence that led investigators to believe they would soon have a long list of suspects. Some detectives were openly surprised by the sloppiness of the raiders. They'd done all the hard work of getting through the wall into the vault brilliantly but then left a bunch of clues in their wake.

Within days, detectives had a list of the most likely suspects for the robbery, and the first alleged robber whose north London home they raided was gang member Danny Jones, 60. Before the Hatton Garden raid, Jones had become obsessed with one particular book called *Forensics for Dummies*, which he believed was essential reading as part of his preparations for the raid. Jones liked to imply he was the technical expert to other members of the gang. In fact, it later emerged that Jones had spent weeks poring over specialist forensic publications and browsing Google for information that might help the gang avoid leaving any significant evidence during the break-in. Jones clearly hadn't read the literature thoroughly enough, because he made a host of elementary mistakes, including not throwing away his mobile and failing to clean the Google search record on his laptop.

At Jones' house in north London, police took away various items, including that computer and a number of mobile "burner" phones, plus that book, *Forensics for Dummies*, along with masks, a walkie-talkie and a magnifying glass. Other members of the Hatton Garden gang later told friends that Jones was more like an overgrown schoolboy than a professional criminal, and he'd clearly pretended to them that he had more knowledge of forensic science than he really did.

Shortly after they'd raided Jones' home, forensic investigators recovered CCTV footage from a number of roadside cameras, which had filmed the gang's vehicles in the area close to the safety deposit centre that was robbed.

As one of the robber's oldest associates later commented: "Leaving all that gear behind was a big mistake, not to mention all the other basic mistakes they also made, like not throwing away phones and laptops. None of them have ever explained why they left in such a hurry and made such a hash of it all. But the aftermath of that job spelt the end for them. What a waste. They'd pulled off the crime of the century and screwed up the next bit."

Seven members of the Hatton Garden gang – with a combined age of more than 500 years – were eventually sentenced to a total of 34 years in jail.

COLD CASES

Thanks to the emergence of DNA fingerprints in the late 1980s, scientists and police investigators eventually found themselves armed with a new tool to try and solve the unsolvable – the cases that had long since been classified as "cold".

Numerous killers had evaded capture for decades thanks to inefficient law enforcement and dated working practices, even within the world of forensic science. Now DNA, combined with other significant new scientific breakthroughs during the 80s and early 90s, convinced law enforcement agents in countries including the UK and US that they stood a realistic chance of solving many horrendous crimes of the past.

All physical evidence containing DNA – blood, semen, hair, saliva and various tissue – is today classified as biological evidence. But back before DNA, more than three decades ago, it was considered as general evidence and mostly kept stored if cases were not solved. Once re-examined, this type of evidence could prove to be a gamechanger, because it was likely to contain DNA which had never before been subjected to a DNA test.

In other words, a lot of potential DNA evidence was sitting untouched and untested in container boxes that had been kept in storage, often for decades. All it required was an inspection of the evidence trays connected to each unsolved case and a gold mine of forensic evidence could be unearthed. Investigators were warned that extracting DNA from old evidence had to be done very carefully because it was often impacted by weather conditions, including heat and moisture. As a result, scientists needed to use specialized techniques, developed to be effective whatever the state of the potential DNA. "The main thing was that it was do-able to reopen cold cases," explained one former London murder detective. "All it needed was the effort to retrieve the evidence taken at the time of the murder and the enquiry could begin all over again."

There were three key elements when it came to reopening cold case enquiries. The first was the DNA databases. In theory, detectives could match up at least half the crimes committed to repeat offenders who'd already submitted their DNA samples into the system after being convicted of any serious offence. "The databases maintained in most countries across the world are probably the single most significant factor when it comes to reopening cold cases and having a realistic chance of finally solving them," said one former Scotland Yard detective.

Secondly, there were new forensic techniques evolving all the time, which could help provide fresh breakthrough evidence for investigators. This ranged from new ways to detect "foreign" materials on a suspect, to being able to more accurately ascertain the time of death of a body in water.

And there was a third reason why cold cases were worth reopening. After long periods of time have elapsed, witnesses and even suspects might be prepared to change their minds about talking for the first time.

On a more personal note, many police officers were keen to relaunch investigations because they wanted to help the families of victims to get closure, sometimes decades after a serious crime was committed. As one former London detective explained: "We knew it could mean reliving many painful details at a trial or hearing. But all the families of the murder victims I've ever known definitely wanted an opportunity to have that sense of closure. Many were even prepared to go through the trauma of listening to all the details of the murder of a loved one in court, just to be able to see the guilty get punished."

Many police officers I've interviewed have told me they've spent years feeling bad about how some of their murder investigations had fizzled out due to a lack of tangible evidence, often much to the disappointment of the victims' families. One recently retired detective explained: "I had at least a dozen unsolved murders that I thought about every day I was working before I retired. I felt so bad about the way we'd let those cases run out of steam. But now there was a fresh chance to bring some of the killers to justice and give the victim's family some sense of closure."

Police, forensics and prosecutors knew only too well that a lot of the offenders brought to justice by reopening cold cases wouldn't always be taken off the streets. Many of them would turn out to already be in prison for other offences, or even dead. "But that's not the point. We always explain to families of victims that this might happen before we reopen any cold case," explained the same recently retired London murder squad detective. "But I don't know one family that said they didn't want us to reopen a cold case. They're desperate for justice, no matter how long after that crime has been committed."

Thousands of cold cases have been brought to a satisfactory conclusion in the US and UK in recent years as a result of highly skilled re-examinations by forensic scientists.

VIKKI THOMPSON

The ability to solve cold case murders thanks to new forensic evidence has played a big role in changing UK laws, when it comes to suspects being tried twice for the same crime. The 1995 killing of mother-of-two Vikki Thompson was one of the first murders to be reinvestigated following changes to UK criminal law that allowed a suspect to be tried twice for certain serious offences, including homicide. It took brand new evidence from forensic scientists to ensure that the retrial even took place.

Vikki, aged 30, had been attacked on 12 August that year near her home in Ascott-under-Wychwood, Oxfordshire, after she stumbled on a man in the middle of masturbating on a deserted country lane. The man battered Vikki with a stone and dragged her body across a field and over two wire fences. Finally, he dumped her by a railway embankment to make it look like she'd been struck by a passing train. Vikki's dog Daisy returned home alone and friends eventually found Vikki semi-conscious and covered in blood, although she was still alive. She tried to talk but wasn't able to identify her attacker. Vikki died in hospital six days later of severe head trauma.

Detectives eventually matched three footprints found near where Vikki had been dumped to a local man called Mark Weston, who lived in the same Oxfordshire village of Ascott-under-Wychwood as his alleged victim. He was arrested and charged with her murder. But at Weston's trial in 1996, the prosecution said he had escaped on foot, leaving those three footprints, which matched his size 12 boots. But the defence argued the prints were made by a smaller shoe. The jury unanimously found Weston not guilty after deliberating for just 50 minutes, on the basis that the prosecution had been unable to show sufficient evidence to prove he was the killer. The foreman of the jury even wrote to Weston after the trial wishing him luck and urged him to pursue the police for compensation.

The police were infuriated. Although they knew for certain that Weston was the killer, they had needed more substantial evidence to successfully prosecute him, and at that time retrials for such offences were not permissible under UK law. The murder remained unsolved for 10 years, until Thames Valley Police decided to launch a cold case review when UK lawmakers announced that in exceptional circumstances suspected murderers could be re-prosecuted if there was sufficient evidence against them.

A team of forensic scientists was brought into the enquiry, and they spent three years working on the case. The key element was a pair of black boots that Weston had been wearing at the time of the murder. They were among the evidence retrieved by the police at the time of the crime. Experts knew blood traces would show up better under fibre optic lamps rather than regular tungsten, which had been used for tests when the murder was first committed.

The forensic team eventually discovered bloodstains – a few millimetres across – on the seams of Weston's boots which matched Vikki Thompson's blood. It was enough for police to issue an arrest warrant for him in October 2009. Weston was quickly detained by officers. He'd always denied knowing the victim or being at the scene on the day of the murder.

At his eventual retrial at Reading Crown Court in 2010, Weston, 35, could not explain how the blood had got onto his boots. Weston was sentenced to life in prison after being found guilty of murdering Vikki Thompson. He was the first person in the United Kingdom to be convicted of murder following the discovery of new forensic evidence.

JOHN COOPER

The ability of detectives to carefully preserve evidence from murders that have remained unsolved for decades is crucial if new advances in forensic science are going to manage to uncover fresh evidence.

In December 1984, Richard Thomas, 58, and his sister Helen, 54, were found murdered at their home, Scoveston Manor, near Milford Haven, in Wales.

Four years later – in June 1989 – married couple Peter Dixon, 51, and his wife Gwenda, 52, were shot in the face with a sawn-off shotgun as they enjoyed a coastal walk on the final day of their Welsh summer holiday on the Pembrokeshire coast. Their killer hid their bodies in nearby bushes and even stole money from them. Within hours he'd used their bank cards to withdraw £300.

These two cold-blooded double murders were to remain unsolved for nearly 20 years, and they struck terror into many who lived in that part of Wales. It was constantly feared that the killer could strike again, at any time, in any place.

For the police, it was particularly frustrating, because they had a chief suspect called John Cooper, then aged 45. He was known to them as a prolific burglar but had avoided arrest for the four murders because of a lack of evidence linking him to the actual crimes.

More than 15 years later – in 2005 – police decided that because of the development of DNA and other new advances in forensic science, it was the right time to reopen this notorious unsolved case. Detectives warned the families of the victims that the killer would not be brought to justice overnight, because there had to be an incredibly detailed re-examination of the evidence taken at the time of both double murders.

Two years later, a breakthrough emerged when traces of victim Peter Dixon's DNA were found on shorts which had earlier been collected by detectives from his home during the original investigation. Police took possession of a gun that main suspect Cooper had used on a later robbery he'd been convicted of. Under microscopic examination, forensic experts found victim Peter Dixon's blood underneath paint on the gun Cooper used in that robbery.

By the time police finally questioned Cooper in April 2009, they were able to link other fibres belonging to him to the killings, the '98 robbery and an attack on a group of teenage girls in which he raped a 16-year-old and sexually assaulted a 15-year-old at gunpoint, also in Pembrokeshire. Forensic investigators re-examined the clothing of the original murder victims as well as other items and uncovered a further complex web of textile fibres, which provided even more powerful links between Cooper and all his alleged victims.

On 26 May 2011, Cooper, from Milford Haven, Pembrokeshire, was given four life sentences for the 1985 double murder of brother and sister Richard and Helen Thomas and the 1989 double murder of Peter and Gwenda Dixon. During his trial, Cooper had even become known as "The Bullseye Killer", because he'd appeared on the TV gameshow *Bullseye* weeks before shooting Peter and Gwenda Dixon dead.

The forensic scientists involved all received formal commendations for their work.

ANDREW EVERSON

Recent new developments in forensic science mean it is now possible to recover miniscule samples of gunshot residue from murders committed decades ago, which would not have been traceable at the time of the offences themselves.

On 14 January 1993, drug dealer David Watkins was executed with a bullet to the back of his head as he stood by his car in Searles Farm Lane, near Reading, in Berkshire. Mr Watkins, a 30-year-old cannabis dealer, had been killed with a shotgun. The murder weapon was never found. Another drug dealer called Andrew Everson was acquitted of the murder by a jury at his 1994 trial after a jury decided there was insufficient evidence that Everson was the killer. Everson had even denied ownership of a shotgun.

Thames Valley Police's major crime review team reopened the case in 2012, convinced that new technology might enable forensics to trace smaller amounts of gunshot residue than before and that that might help them finally solve the case. A team of forensic investigators spent months carrying out tests, which eventually confirmed Everson was connected to the gunshot residue found in his car. This meant he must have been handling the gun hours before Mr Watkins' murder. As a result, Everson's original acquittal was quashed by the Court of Appeal and a retrial was ordered.

At Everson's new 2019 trial, prosecutor John Price QC told the court that the "small but detectable" amount of gunshot residue was found in vacuumed samples of Everson's vehicle, which had been collected back at the time of the killing. Everson's claim that he wasn't present at the time of the murder crumbled when the court was presented with additional scientific proof, thanks to infrared devices used by forensics to expose organic compounds left at the crime scene, that linked Everson to the car, as well as to those gunshot particles.

The court heard that Everson had 118 previous convictions for a range of crimes, including violence and possession of firearms and ammunition. Everson was eventually found unanimously guilty of killing David Watkins. The judge told the defendant he'd be serving a minimum term of 27 years. As he was sentenced, Everson shouted from the dock: "I didn't kill him, all I did was sell him some fucking puff."

STEPHEN LAWRENCE

The significance of a murder case can be underestimated during the early days of an enquiry. That's when sloppy – or sometimes even corrupt – detective work results in glaring omissions which can impact forensic evidence and prevent the guilty parties being brought to justice.

On a mild spring night on 22 April 1993 in Well Hall, Eltham, south-east London, teenager Stephen Lawrence – from nearby Plumstead – was viciously stabbed to death in an unprovoked, racially motivated attack by a gang of white youths while he waited with his friend Duwayne Brooks at a bus stop.

Over the days that followed, police received several tip-offs naming the most likely suspects for the killing of the

18-year-old as brothers Neil and Jamie Acourt, Gary Dobson and David Norris. Three days later, officers even took a statement from the alleged victim of another stabbing committed by the same suspects. Despite seeming to already have enough evidence to make arrests, police instead launched a surveillance operation on the four suspects' homes. At one stage, officers saw them walking out of a house carrying bin bags and driving away. The police investigators did not follow them because – they later claimed – they didn't have a mobile phone with which to call their commanding officer for his orders.

One of the suspects, David Norris, was in fact the son of a local criminal called Clifford Norris, who would eventually be alleged to have corrupt connections to a number of south London police officers. Clifford Norris's family members claimed Norris senior regularly used his police connections to protect himself, his criminal associates and his close relations from justice.

One south London detective later explained: "I hate to say this but, from an initial standpoint, this case should have been relatively simple. As with so many stab wounds cases, if it had been a millimetre one way or the other, Stephen could so easily just have ended up in hospital for a couple of days. But he didn't. However, forensic evidence was crucial in order to connect the suspects with the murder and that was not forthcoming. Then there were complex issues that meant there was a complete lack of a fully fledged police investigation and that had huge long-term implications."

The majority of detectives involved in the Stephen Lawrence murder enquiry didn't realize that Clifford Norris's south London crime boss was already pulling the strings on the case from his nearby prison cell, where he was serving a sentence for his role in handling the proceeds from one of Britain's biggest ever robberies. This same crime boss knew full well that his connections to detectives in south-east London was a potential source of power and influence. He believed that if he could help get the Lawrence murder investigation dropped, it would protect the son of one of his henchmen and be something he could always hold over any corrupt officers on his payroll, whenever they stepped out of line.

But when the five white youths suspected of killing Stephen Lawrence never ended up being charged, London's Metropolitan Police would eventually end up being accused of institutional racism on the basis that they did not try hard enough to solve the murder because of the victim's colour.

The case rumbled on for 11 years without any of the suspects being brought to justice. There were public enquiries and many attempts to reopen the case, but they all failed to result in the arrest of the alleged killers. Just as it seemed the trail that led to Stephen Lawrence's killers had gone cold, forensic scientists were approached to review the evidence down to the smallest detail. So it was that, in 2006, a 15-strong forensic team started working on Stephen Lawrence's 1993 murder. Their investigation was to take a total of five years and cost many millions of pounds.

The scientists were asked to re-examine every piece of evidence connected to the Stephen Lawrence murder. The scientists' strategy was simple. They were going to look for *anything at all* that could have been transferred from Stephen Lawrence to any of the men the police believed killed him. First, they had to go through the lengthy and intricate process of checking that none of the evidence they intended to examine had in any way been cross-contaminated during those forensic tests at the time of the murder itself. As one forensic scientist closely connected to the Lawrence case later explained: "In cold cases, there are three possibilities: there's nothing there, it was missed, or it wasn't looked for. You have to start from scratch, assume nothing and that's exactly what they did on the Stephen Lawrence case."

But the path to forensic discoveries and justice wasn't going to be an easy one. Other forensic scientists had worked on and off the case from 1995 onwards, and naturally the new team were reluctant to cast any judgements on their fellow scientists. In fact, this was another reason why they'd decided it was imperative to start the process right from scratch. It was later alleged that certain fibre samples had been missed at the time of the original investigation because of the inferior equipment available to forensic scientists. This was said to have made uncovering such small samples akin to "looking for a needle in a haystack". But it was hoped that advances in profiling during the intervening years would prove to be a crucial factor in discovering new evidence and securing convictions.

The team of forensic experts first began with a detailed analysis of the clothes Stephen Lawrence had been wearing on the day he was murdered. They followed this up with a careful examination of the garments the police had seized from the suspects. A jacket belonging to suspect Dobson had first been analyzed back at the time of the murder in 1993. DNA profiling had been in its infancy back then, and a slight stain of blood found by examiners had been considered too small to provide an acceptable DNA test sample.

The new forensic team re-examined the inside of the back of the neck of suspect Dobson's jacket and found that same minute blood stain, which measured approximately 0.5 by 0.3 millimetres. DNA profiling using the latest equipment immediately flagged up the blood as matching Stephen Lawrence's profile.

But this new team of forensic investigators weren't finished yet. A further microscopic search turned up further evidence that one forensic expert later said was akin to finding an earring on a football pitch. They discovered several tiny pieces of cut hair on the suspects' clothing that matched Stephen Lawrence's hair.

The forensic team continued their examinations knowing they still had a long way to go before they could present all this evidence. Their evidence had to be as bullet-proof as possible because of the high-profile nature of the case. Also, the team of investigators did not want to put Stephen Lawrence's parents through any more trauma than they had already experienced following the huge public outcry over their son's unsolved, racially motivated murder.

Scientists found red fibres on Stephen's jacket, which could have come from his polo shirt. The examiners pondered on whether it was possible those fibres could have been transferred onto the attackers' clothes. The forensic team then uncovered the same red polycotton fibres from Stephen's jacket on suspect Gary Dobson's jacket, as well as on fellow suspect Stephen Norris's sweatshirt. They widened their search and found more fibres from Stephen Lawrence's jacket on Dobson's jacket and cardigan. There were fibres from Stephen's trousers on Norris's sweatshirt.

The forensic team carried out a second blood test on one of the fibres from Stephen's shirt that had earlier been found on Dobson's jacket. This time the test involved shining different wavelengths of light through fibres and measuring what emerged the other side. One piece of fibre reconfirmed the earlier findings that it was on Dobson's jacket. There were blood flakes present, including one with a couple of fibres in it. Those fibres not only matched Stephen Lawrence's cardigan but tests confirmed it was the dead teenager's blood. Two more hairs were found in the evidence bag containing Norris's jeans, one of which matched Mr Lawrence's DNA to a probability of one in a thousand, and six fibres on his sweatshirt could have come from the victim's trousers.

The forensic investigators set out to try and find more blood on suspect Dobson's jacket. Eventually, using a low-powered microscope, the team found a second minute, near-invisible stain on the back of the collar. It matched Stephen's blood. This was the penultimate breakthrough, because it was what is known in the world of forensic science as a "wet blood stain". This put the jacket at the scene of the murder, or a short time thereafter.

Suspects Dobson, now 36, and Norris, now 35, finally went to trial for the murder of Stephen Lawrence in late 2011. Both denied murder. The trial was the second time Dobson had appeared at the Old Bailey in connection with the murder. In the past, this could not have happened, because of the double jeopardy rule, which prevented a suspect being tried a second time for crimes such as murder. But the law was changed in 2003 to allow a prosecution to go ahead if a court was satisfied there was new and compelling evidence to be put before a jury.

The hearing revolved around those blood spots and flecks, as well as fibres and hairs found on the suspects' clothing. The prosecution insisted that the evidence proved the two men were among the violent gang who'd stabbed Stephen Lawrence to death after racially taunting him. The defence insisted the forensic findings were nothing more than a "teaspoon" of evidence, because of potential cross-contamination of forensic evidence over the years. Experts subsequently gave expert testimony insisting this was not the case and provided testimony about how tests were carried out which proved links between the defendants and Stephen Lawrence. The trial heard there was only a one-in-a-billion chance that a bloodstain found on Gary Dobson's clothing didn't belong to Stephen Lawrence. During cross-examination, one defending barrister produced a damning report from a senior police officer made in 1999 which questioned "the deterioration of the packaging of the clothing exhibits in this case".

Dobson and Norris admitted in court to becoming angry men who'd grown to resent the world after being spat at and verbally abused on a regular basis by members of the public who saw them as murderers. They both gave testimony from the stand to try and disprove any connection to a killing that had come to define their lives. But this time they failed to convince the jury, and both men were found guilty of murder following their six-week trial, which had hinged on that new scientific evidence.

The following day both men were jailed for life. Gary Dobson would serve a minimum of 15 years and 2 months, and David Norris 14 years and 3 months. Passing sentence, the judge, Mr Justice Treacy, described the crime as a "murder which scarred the conscience of the nation".

RACHEL NICKELL

A catalogue of errors by police investigators can take a murder enquiry in entirely the wrong direction. Forensic clues are ignored as detectives become obsessed with bringing a supposedly guilty person to justice. In these trying circumstances, it often ends up being the forensic scientists who finally ensure that the real offenders are prosecuted.

The murder of young mother Rachel Nickell stunned and horrified the British public. On a summer's morning in

July 1992, the 23-year-old was stabbed 49 times and sexually assaulted as she walked through Wimbledon Common with her two-year-old son and the family dog. It appeared to have been a frenzied attack by a complete stranger. There were no witnesses except Rachel's distraught two-year-old son Alex, who was later found by a dog walker clinging to his mother's blood-soaked body.

So began one of the most problematic investigations ever carried out by London's Metropolitan Police. Initially, detectives identified a 29-year-old unemployed local man called Colin Stagg – a frequent visitor to the common while walking his dog – as their number one suspect. Detectives had little more than a hunch to go on at that stage, so they launched "Operation Ezdell" in order to prove Stagg was Rachel's killer. An undercover policewoman attempted to get information from Stagg by pretending to be romantically interested in him. The pair regularly met up, had numerous phone conversations and even exchanged letters containing sexual fantasies. As Stagg gradually developed a trust in the undercover officer, he confessed to his own violent fantasies. He never actually admitted to murdering Rachel Nickell, though. After police had secretly recorded a meeting between the female officer and Stagg, detectives were sanctioned by the Crown Prosecution Service to arrest Stagg and charge him with Rachel's murder.

At the eventual trial, it was revealed that the police evidence was far from concrete. Stagg continued to deny any involvement in the Wimbledon Common murder, and it became apparent during the trial that the police attempt to entrap Stagg had left huge holes in the case against him. Eventually, the judge presiding over the case ruled that the police had shown "excessive zeal" and accused them of trying to incriminate Stagg by "deceptive conduct of the grossest kind". Every aspect of the police's entrapment evidence was dismissed, and the prosecution was forced to withdraw their case. Colin Stagg was formally acquitted in September 1994.

The Metropolitan Police were deeply embarrassed by the failed prosecution of Colin Stagg for Rachel's murder. For a couple of years, they behaved as if they simply wanted it to go away, and some officers still insisted that Stagg was guilty, despite the judge's comments at his earlier trial. The media and some of the victim's family members seriously impacted by the police's failure to catch the Wimbledon Common murderer began to voice their anger at the Metropolitan force's complete failure to bring the killer to justice.

Finally, in 2001 – seven years after Stagg's acquittal – Scotland Yard announced they were going to re-examine evidence gathered at the time of Rachel's murder from the crime scene and use some of the latest advances in forensic technology to study every relevant item. The first forensic laboratory to look at the material found nothing because the samples they'd been provided with by the police had been "inhibited" by the way they'd been handled at the time of the original investigation. The lab in question insisted this had resulted in a chemical imbalance, which would cause any new DNA tests to fail.

When this news was publicly revealed, it caused outrage, and there were even allegations that the police had deliberately "damaged" the evidence because they were so embarrassed by their earlier failure to solve the case.

The pressure became so intense that Scotland Yard eventually had no choice but to ask another forensic laboratory to review the case evidence, and the cold case was officially reopened for a second time.

More significant improvements in the DNA testing system had just come into force, so this was used on traces of DNA found on Rachel's body. The murder itself was completely re-evaluated in a bid to identify certain patterns of behaviour exhibited during the attack, which might provide further clues as to the identity of the real killer of Rachel Nickell. Investigators pledged to look further afield to see if her murder could be connected to any other similar killings.

Samples taken from Rachel Nickell's body were eventually analyzed using a specialized technique known as Low Copy Number DNA. This was supposed to amplify minute quantities of DNA evidence to allow a match to be found but, as in the earlier test, this technique failed. The new forensic team examining the Rachel Nickell case decided to dilute a renegade DNA sample they had recovered back down to its original level. That resulted in a mixed DNA profile, which contained a minor male component, which had to belong to her killer. And that sample of DNA did not match Colin Stagg's. The same lab verified that this latest DNA profile was 1.4 million times more likely to have come from a known serial killer called Robert

Napper. He'd been an original suspect, who had actually failed twice to provide DNA samples to police.

The new team of investigators noticed similarities between the Nickell case and a double murder carried out in May 1994 by Napper. Just 16 months after Nickell's murder, Napper had been convicted for the murder and sexual assault of a mother and her four-year-old daughter. Napper had been sent to the maximum-security psychiatric hospital Broadmoor for that other double murder, a rape and two attempted rapes. He was suspected of being the "Green Chain Rapist", who'd carried out numerous sex attacks in south-east London in the early 1990s.

But the DNA sample was not considered "safe enough" evidence to convict Napper. The forensic team working on the Rachel Nickell case examined hair combings taken from her toddler son Alex and found flakes of red paint that would eventually be matched to a toolbox found at Napper's home.

Finally, the forensic team reconstructed some of the events of the day of the murder on Wimbledon Common itself. At one stage, forensic scientists got down on their hands and knees on the common and were able to establish that the kind of shoes Napper had been wearing, in those ground conditions, could leave prints smaller than the heels themselves, just like the prints left on the path near where Rachel was murdered.

In their search for "foreign DNA" that could have come from Rachel's attacker, a scientist even put on clothes similar to Rachel's. Another colleague acted as the attacker. With black powder applied to his hands, he pulled and pushed them until they resembled the distribution of Rachel's clothing when her body was found. Residues of black powder indicated where contact had been greatest and where the team should focus their testing. This approach revealed further male DNA on Rachel's clothing which had been missed during the original investigation and which turned out to match DNA from Robert Napper.

On 18 December 2008, Robert Napper pleaded guilty to the manslaughter of Rachel Nickell on the grounds of diminished responsibility, due to his diagnosed paranoid schizophrenia. He was sent back to Broadmoor hospital indefinitely. Police eventually examined 106 other offences involving 86 victims regarding offences they believed could be connected to Napper.

Detectives have since been forced to admit they should have arrested Robert Napper – who also suffered from Asperger's Syndrome – much sooner, and possibly even *before* he killed Nickell and those two other victims.

It was then disclosed that, years before the Wimbledon Common attack, Napper's own mother had contacted the police to say her son had committed a rape. But she'd provided the wrong location – Plumstead Common instead of a house in the Plumstead area – and officers never managed to trace the crime she claimed her son had committed.

Police went on to release a public apology to Colin Stagg for his wrongful conviction. It did little to cover up the series of errors and poor police work that had been initially carried out, and, once again, forensic evidence proved pivotal in solving a notorious cold case murder enquiry.

DAMILOLA TAYLOR

The police often find themselves in the firing line when it comes to accusations of allowing the guilty to escape justice. But sometimes forensic scientists have also been known to make some very costly mistakes.

At 4.51 p.m. on 27 November 2000, 10-year-old schoolboy Damilola Taylor set off from Peckham Library, in south London, to walk home. He was filmed on CCTV happily skipping along the pavement as he approached the North Peckham Estate where he lived. Moments later, three boys, aged 12, 13 and 14, tried to steal Damilola's silver Puffa jacket, the only item of value he had on him. During a scuffle, a broken bottle punctured the left part of Damilola's thigh, which severed an artery. Staggering to a stairwell, the schoolboy collapsed bleeding profusely as emergency services rushed to the scene. Damilola was still alive when an ambulance picked him up some minutes later. He died minutes after he arrived at hospital. It was 10 days before his eleventh birthday.

The killing of an innocent 10-year-old boy in south London shocked the nation and has never been forgotten. As one journalist wrote in 2006: "That CCTV footage showed a happy smiling schoolboy hopping and skipping, with the insuppressible exuberance of childhood, across the flagstones of a shopping precinct. It was Peckham but it could have been anywhere in Britain."

Crucial evidence identifying the alleged killers of Damilola was missed by forensic scientists in the days following the killing. In 2002, the three suspects were all acquitted of involvement in the death of the 10-year-old schoolboy.

Fast forward four years to 2006, and a brand-new team of forensic scientists was tasked with uncovering fresh evidence that, it was hoped, would lead to a retrial of the accused boys. Forensic scientists faced an uphill task from the moment they got involved. As a result, this new forensic team made the time-consuming decision to re-examine every piece of relevant evidence they had access to. Many months later, scientists found a bloodstain on the heel of one suspect's trainer. They also discovered a much smaller stain on the cuff of his brother's sweatshirt. Both samples of blood belonged to Damilola Taylor. As one member of the new forensic team later explained: "The police got a lot of flack when the suspects were originally acquitted, but in fact the forensic scientists who first worked on the case had missed a blood stain on the back of a pair of trainers that matched Damilola's DNA."

The new team of forensic scientists uncovered a textile fibre embedded in an item belonging to one of the suspects that matched fibres from Damilola's jumper. This meant it must have been transferred when the blood was wet. A fibre from the trousers Damilola was wearing at the time of the attack was found within that blood spot. Another speck of

Damilola's blood was recovered from the cuff of a sweatshirt belonging to one of the suspects.

One of the scientists who discovered this new evidence later told a court that human error by the original forensic investigators most likely occurred because gathering evidence is such a painstaking process that it was relatively easy to mislay such evidence.

The new team of forensic scientists presented to the court alternative events that could have led to Damilola Taylor's fatal wounds. The theory eventually accepted by the court was that he was attacked and fell on a broken bottle, later bleeding to death. The time-consuming work of the new forensic team eventually helped convict two teenage brothers for the manslaughter of Damilola nearly six years after their original acquittal. They were each given eight years' in youth custody.

MILLY DOWLER

Forensic evidence from the scenes of all murders – including cold cases – can come in all shapes and sizes. Some breakthrough evidence is traced by low-key technical experts, who rarely get mentioned outside of their laboratories, even though they've played a crucial role in finding a killer.

Thirteen-year-old Milly Dowler disappeared while walking home from a suburban station in Surrey, on the outskirts of south London, on 21 March 2002. She'd just travelled by train from nearby Heathside School in Weybridge. That day, Milly had intended on going straight back to her parents' home in nearby Hersham, but she and a friend got off a stop earlier at Walton-on-Thames. The pair made their way to a café for a bite to eat, and at 3:47 p.m. Milly called her dad to say she'd be home in half an hour. At 4:05 p.m. the girls left the cafe and went their separate ways. The last person to see Milly alive was a friend of her sister's standing at a nearby bus stop.

Further down the road from the cafe was a CCTV camera, which never captured an image of the schoolgirl. But it did film a blurred image of a red car that belonged to a local woman, which was being driven by her boyfriend, a man called Levi Bellfield, at the time.

At 7 p.m. that same evening, Milly was reported missing after she failed to return home. A nationwide search was sparked, with widespread appeals to find the girl, as more than 100 police officers and helicopters searched nearby streets, fields and rivers. Despite all those efforts, by June of that year there had been no trace of Milly, and the police informed her heartbroken parents that their daughter was most likely dead.

Three months later – on 18 September 2002 – her remains were discovered in the woods in Yateley Heath, 25 miles away from Walton, where she had disappeared all those months earlier. Initially, forensic scientists were unable to say exactly how Milly died, because her body was so badly decomposed. She was eventually identified through her dental records.

Levi Bellfield – the man whose distorted image was caught on CCTV driving that red car close to where Milly disappeared – emerged as the police's number one suspect after the same car was linked to an attempted abduction just 24 hours before Milly went missing. Detectives knew he was most likely the killer, but they could do nothing about it unless they came up with a confirmed sighting of him in the street at the same time as Milly. There had been no other evidence, including DNA, to match Bellfield to the murder, and – despite repeated public appeals for witnesses – the case eventually went cold.

For eight years, detectives failed to find a reason to reopen the investigation. Frustratingly, they remained convinced that Bellfield had killed Milly Dowler, but they had no evidence with which to mount a prosecution. However, forensic science is not just about meticulously recreating crime scenes or experimenting with test tubes or taking samples of DNA. There are many other potential ways to uncover crucial evidence. That's when detectives turned to digital imaging expert and former RAF officer Andy Laws, who specialized in identifying people from distorted, poor quality CCTV and photographic images.

Firstly, Andy Laws was able to match the red car in the relevant CCTV footage as definitely being the same vehicle seen being driven by Levi Bellfield. Laws even managed to improve the quality of the footage to such an extent that Bellfield's image became much clearer to see. Knowing the identity of the driver of that car was just one small step in the investigation to try and bring Bellfield to justice all those years after the murder of Milly Dowler.

Andy Laws' next challenge was to try and establish if it was possible to walk down the street where Bellfield lived (and Milly disappeared) and avoid being filmed by two rotating, unsynchronized CCTV cameras mounted at either end of an overlooking office building. If it wasn't, this meant Milly disappeared before she passed the camera. Levi Bellfield's flat was halfway along that same street, behind a hedge.

Investigators knew from the earlier eyewitness – who'd seen Milly in the street that afternoon – that she'd been about 50 yards from that precise location when she was last seen. Expert Andy Laws eventually established that, despite trees and traffic in that street and the glare of lights from a car park, it wasn't possible to avoid those CCTV cameras. This meant Millie must have been abducted during that 50-yard walk. Andy Laws was able to prove it wasn't possible for a car to stop on that street and pick someone up without being filmed. That meant whoever attacked her must live on that same street.

The expert's next task was to trace and identify every person who passed those cameras during the 30-minute window when Milly disappeared. In all, there were 98 people. Eventually, all of them were discounted from being involved. Police now knew they had enough evidence to arrest Levi Bellfield.

As another digital imaging expert later explained: "The real high in a job like ours is presenting the evidence and letting it speak in the truest way possible. That's when both sides say: 'Yes.' That's the buzz."

On 23 June 2011, Levi Bellfield – already serving three life sentences for the murders of Marsha McDonnell and Amélie

Delagrange and the attempted murder of Kate Sheedy – was found guilty of abducting and murdering Milly Dowler and sentenced to an additional whole-life tariff. Five years later, Bellfield bragged to a fellow prison inmate that he had had an accomplice when he murdered Milly Dowler and admitted some of the details behind his attack on the schoolgirl. When police heard about Bellfield's sick boasts they confronted Bellfield, who finally confessed to what he had done to Milly after having at first dismissed the other inmate's claims as having being fabricated to impress a fellow prisoner.

On 27 January 2016, Surrey Police publicly announced that Bellfield had finally admitted to abducting, abusing and killing the schoolgirl. The 47-year-old killer told detectives he'd abducted Milly and first assaulted her at his flat close to Walton railway station. After that, he took her to the driveway of his mother's nearby home where he raped her in broad daylight over the boot of his car.

Detectives later announced that they believed Bellfield may have been responsible for around 20 other attacks on women which were never solved.

WORLD'S END MURDERS

Forensic scientists are not great believers in fate. They deal in facts and scientific data most of the time, and pride themselves on leaving the guesswork to others. But occasionally even these often-detached characters can find themselves emotionally drawn into a case through no fault of their own.

In October 1977, student Lorna Dawson was studying geography at Edinburgh University, in Scotland, when two teenagers – Helen Scott and Christine Eadie – were brutally murdered after a night out at the city's World's End pub. The 17-year-olds had been beaten, gagged, tied, raped and strangled. Their naked and battered bodies were dumped in plain sight. "They were discarded like department store mannequins," Lorna later recalled. "These were gruesome, callous murders. Helen and Christine were just innocent girls enjoying a fun night out, who were in the wrong place at the wrong time." Lorna Dawson was a country girl who'd been brought up on a farm and was new to Scotland's capital city. So this shocking crime seemed all the more disturbing when Lorna realized she could so easily have been a victim herself, as the girls lived very near her student digs.

Despite a massive police manhunt, the World's End murder case was scaled down after a year and no one was charged. The killer remained at large. Lorna never forgot the case, though. She later recalled: "It felt so unfair that the killer could get away with such a horrible crime, particularly when you could see the anguish that the families of the victims were going through."

After completing a PhD in soil science, Lorna initially applied her specialist knowledge to projects relating to agriculture and the environment.

In 2003, police asked her to help examine a spade found in a suspected drug dealer's car. She managed to link soil samples to a nearby wood, where a stash of illegal narcotics was found.

Now Professor Dawson, Lorna would end up running one of the world's only laboratories dedicated to forensic soil science. It's called the James Hutton Institute, in Aberdeen, Scotland. By this time, soil evidence was regularly leading investigators to bodies and had helped overturn many criminals' alibis. It had even been used to help uncover the origins of stolen artefacts. Lorna Dawson went on to work on more than 70 criminal cases from around the globe over a 15-year period.

In 2005, Scottish police charged a man called Angus Sinclair with the murder and rape of Helen Scott and Christine Eadie, the World's End murder victims. Two years later, his trial collapsed due to a lack of evidence. Seven years after that – in 2014 – Professor Lorna Dawson found herself drawn back into the World's End murder investigation when she was approached by prosecutors to help solve this notorious cold case once and for all. Professor Dawson later described their approach as feeling as if her life had "come full circle".

Her ground-breaking forensic techniques included a specialized strategy, which involved combining inorganic characterizations of material, which then enabled her and her team to examine a wide range of trace evidence.

As a result, Professor Dawson was able to analyze tiny soil particles taken from Helen Scott's feet and establish that they matched soil particles taken from the suspected killer. This would play a crucial role in helping to convict Sinclair for the murders.

He was eventually sentenced to life imprisonment with a minimum term of 37 years – meaning he would have to live to 106 to ever be eligible for parole. Now considered to be Scotland's worst serial killer, Sinclair is believed to have killed at least another six women during his twisted reign of terror.

Following the final trial, victim Helen Scott's father, Morain, thanked Professor Lorna Dawson for her work that helped bring his daughter's killer to justice. He'd carried the burden of his daughter's murder his entire life. Lorna later explained: "I could see his relief at finally getting some sort of closure."

ANDREW PENNINGTON

Police in the UK are at pains to emphasize that it's not just cold case murders that they reopen thanks to DNA and other developments in forensic science.

In 2017, Cleveland and North Yorkshire Major Investigation Team detectives believed that advances in forensic science relating to DNA testing would help them to identify the perpetrator of a 1988 rape.

Forensic investigators extracted samples from the available evidence taken at the time of the offence and found the same man had committed three house burglaries in 1997. Detectives eventually matched those samples on the DNA database to a man called Andrew Pennington. Back in 1988, he'd been aged 24 and was working as a forklift truck driver while living in Howden, near Goole, in North Yorkshire. Pennington had been out for an evening in York city centre on Saturday 29 October that year. He was walking back through the Castlegate area towards his car when he approached a 27-year-old woman – whom he'd never met. When she tried to ignore him, he pushed her into a building and raped her before fleeing the area.

Ten years later Pennington committed three house burglaries in Beverley, Yorkshire, stealing jewellery, electrical items and both ladies' and children's underwear. Once again, he got away with his crimes.

During police interviews following Pennington's arrest after the discovery of his DNA match, Pennington admitted carrying out the attack and the burglaries and even told officers: "I've been expecting this one day."

He was charged with rape and a section 14 indecent assault under the Sexual Offences Act, to which he subsequently pleaded guilty. In March 2018, Pennington – aged 53 – was jailed for a total of 10 years after admitting all the offences.

JAMES BEN DAVIES

Familial DNA testing introduced in the UK in the late 1990s meant that scientists could match a suspect's DNA to family members in a bid to track down an offender if that DNA could not be matched on the UK database. One of the first cases that used this specialized technique revolved around the 1998 hunt for a man suspected of committing three violent sexual assaults on women in the UK.

The first sexual assault had occurred in Farnborough, Hampshire, on 20 February 1998 at 8.45 p.m. A 20-year-old woman was walking along a dimly lit street when she was pushed to the floor and attacked. On 14 August 1998 at 3.20 p.m., a 32-year-old woman was assaulted while walking her dog on waste-ground in the village of Eaton Socon, in Cambridgeshire. The third sexual assault took place at 2 p.m. on 12 January 2000 in the village of Bozeat, Northamptonshire. A 40-year-old woman was walking her dog when a man jogged towards her, pushed her into a hedgerow and attacked her.

Police and forensic investigators managed to recover DNA samples from each attack, so they knew the attacks were all the work of one man, but they could not find any match for the DNA from the UK database. With no other concrete leads, police from the three different UK regions where the rapist had struck agreed to jointly fund a familial DNA search on the samples obtained from each of the crime scenes. Eventually they turned up a match to one particular family, some of whose members had logged their DNA on the UK database after committing a wide range of crimes.

As a result of these findings, police officers from Hampshire, Cambridgeshire and Surrey began a number of intelligence-led enquiries to try and narrow down the likely identity of the actual rapist in all three attacks. After interviewing various members of the same family, they were told that the most likely suspect was a man called James Ben Davies, who lived in Surrey. He was closely related to one of the people detectives had contacted.

On 17 August 2000, Davies was arrested at his home. He was eventually sentenced to four and a half years in prison after pleading guilty to all three of those sexual assaults.

This case was especially significant because its success-ful conclusion meant that investigators now knew that the familial DNA system was highly efficient. It meant forensic scientists and detectives now had another weapon in their armoury when it came to tracking down criminals. The Forensic Science Service – who helped pioneer familial DNA testing – said at the time: "This is a real breakthrough in the investigation of serial offenders who operate in differ-ent locations. The FSS provided the springboard which the combined police investigation carried forward to today's conviction." One detective involved in the Davies investi-gation was equally delighted by the success of the familial DNA system. The officer said: "The sentencing of James Ben Davies today marks the end of an extensive and thorough investigation involving three police forces. The successful conclusion of this case is thanks to developments in foren-sic science surrounding DNA, together with detailed intelli-gence-led police inquiries."

GLADYS GODFREY

With one successful familial DNA-led prosecution under their belt, law makers in the UK felt confident enough to start using the system to try and track down cold case murderers.

The killing of elderly Gladys Godfrey in September 2002 in Mansfield, Nottinghamshire, left residents in her commu-nity in fear. The sheer brutality of the slaying even shocked the most seasoned detectives investigating the case. Gladys had left her detached home unlocked, and police later concluded that this enabled a man to enter her bungalow, where he raped and beat the 87-year-old widow to death in a chair in her living room, where she often slept at night because she was convinced that if she used her bed she might die in it.

Incredibly, the same man had broken into Gladys's house 18 months earlier – in April 2001 – and knocked her to the floor, before exposing himself. During that attack, Gladys – 4 foot 11 inches tall and weighing just 6 stone – had managed to defend herself and even hit the man with a lemonade bottle. He eventually fled after taking her handbag. Sixteen months later, the same man beat and stamped on Gladys before kicking her viciously and finally strangling her so violently that he pulled out clumps of her hair. The old lady's injuries included a fractured skull and broken neck. Her face and body were in such a distressing state that her niece was not allowed to identify the body.

Forensic investigators took a sample of the killer's DNA from the murder scene and found it matched DNA samples from the earlier attack, so they knew they were looking for one man responsible for both crimes. Efforts to trace the killer through his DNA profile drew a blank because the man had never been arrested. This meant he wasn't on the National DNA Database. Police took swabs from 1,100 men in the Mansfield area close to Gladys's home to try and track down the killer, but there were no matches. That's when forensic scientists turned to their recently developed familial DNA testing system. This eventually provided detectives with a long list of relatives – all in the nearby Nottingham area – who were connected through the DNA samples found at the scene of the murder and the earlier violent attack.

There were no obvious suspects among them, so detectives refined their list geographically and came up with 10 likely suspects for investigators to interview in the actual city of Nottingham, who'd all come up on the familial DNA match. The second name on that list told police the name of the relative of his who was most likely to be responsible. This led detectives to Jason Ward, who lived in Bentinck Street, just a mile and a half away from Gladys's home in Devon Drive.

Ward immediately agreed to have his DNA taken and it matched the samples from the original crime scenes. Ward's fingerprints matched those found at Gladys's bungalow.

He was a loner who lived with his parents, spent much of his time playing computer games and had problems with alcohol and solvent abuse. One former classmate said at the time he was "strange, weird and easily led". Ward initially denied killing Gladys. Faced with all the forensic evidence, he eventually pleaded guilty to rape and murder and was given a life sentence with a minimum term of 22 years.

It was the first-ever successful murder conviction which had used the familial DNA searching system to track down a killer.

COLETTE ARAM

Familial DNA testing has gone on to be used on multiple UK cold case murder enquiries, as law enforcement realize it gives them a much better chance of bringing the guilty to justice. One London murder squad detective explained: "Familial DNA was a huge step forward for police investigating cold cases. It was a viable route to catching a criminal, which hadn't existed before." Unsolved murder cases going back decades are now said by detectives to be 50 per cent more solvable, thanks to DNA and in particular the familial testing process.

On 30 October 1983, 16-year-old British trainee hair-dresser Colette Aram was abducted, raped and strangled while walking from her home to her boyfriend's house in Keyworth, Nottinghamshire. It was a frustrating case for detectives because they simply didn't have enough evidence to arrest their chief suspect Paul Hutchinson, and the case eventually ran out of steam.

Twenty-five years later, in June 2008, Hutchinson's son Jean-Paul was arrested for a motoring offence. A routine swab was taken from the younger man – who was only 20 at the time of his arrest – and he came up as having a familial DNA link to the DNA sample taken from the body of Colette Aram. Jean-Paul hadn't even been born at the time of the murder, so forensic scientists switched their attention to his close relatives and soon realized that his father was the man who'd been considered the main suspect in the killing of Colette all those years earlier.

Paul Stewart Hutchinson – by this time aged 50 – was arrested. His DNA matched that recovered from the murder scene and he was charged with the murder in April 2009. Hutchinson entered a plea of not guilty on 5 October. Facing undeniable DNA and other forensic evidence, he changed his plea to guilty at a pre-trial hearing on 21 December that same year. Two weeks later, Hutchinson was jailed for life with a minimum of 25 years at Nottingham Crown Court for the murder of Colette Aram.

Colette's mother Jacqui Kirkby said Hutchinson's sentencing brought some relief, although the family still needed to know why Colette was killed – a question Hutchinson refused to answer.

On 11 October 2010, Hutchinson was found unconscious in his cell at Nottingham Prison. He died in an ambulance on the way to hospital. It is believed he took an overdose of medication, but a post-mortem examination was inconclusive.

MELANIE HALL

Detectives throughout the UK started to reopen further cold case murder enquiries now that they felt confident of solving these crimes, thanks to familial DNA. The 1984 murder of teenager Melanie Hall in Bath, Somerset, England, had remained unsolved for 30 years, but the police were determined not to let the case simply slip into oblivion.

Back at the time of the killing, police had collected blood and other relevant evidence from an alleyway called St

Stephen's Court, where Melanie's body had been discovered in a pool of blood at 5.30 a.m. on 9 June 1984. She'd been stabbed 26 times through her clothing. The killer had then stripped her naked and raped her, before placing all the clothes back on her body. More blood was found nearby that led from the murder location in the direction of a local man's home half a mile away. He'd become the police's number one suspect, but detectives were warned by prosecutors that they would need much more evidence than that to pin it on the man.

Officers from Avon and Somerset Police meticulously took swabs from 71 blood spots at the scene, as well as from victim Melanie's clothing and body. But no other tangible evidence emerged which could be used to warrant arresting their main suspect. As a result, detectives and their forensic colleagues meticulously stored away boxes containing the samples and evidence collected from the scene of the murder. They would remain in storage until police felt they had a chance to bring their main suspect to justice.

Ten years after Melanie's murder, a DNA profile of the killer was successfully extracted from samples of semen found at the scene at the time of the murder. This was loaded onto the UK's national DNA database by investigators, hopeful that they might finally be able to prosecute their original suspect. But no DNA match came up on the database at that time. Detectives presumed the killer had either never been arrested for any criminal offences or perhaps was dead. The investigation into Melanie's murder ended up being put on ice for a further 20 years.

In 2014, a 41-year-old woman's DNA was put into the UK's standard national database following a domestic incident with her partner. A year later, the same woman's DNA was re-entered into a new, more sophisticated version of the UK's DNA database, and it threw up a familial DNA link to the murder of teenager Melanie Hall almost 30 years earlier. Detectives knew immediately that the woman could not have been involved in the killing because she wasn't old enough. But they noted that her father Christopher Hampton *had* been that suspect whose trail of blood had been found near the original 1984 murder scene.

As a result of that "hit" detectives decided to approach Hampton for a sample of his own DNA. On 1 June 2015, he voluntarily provided a mouth swab to them. Hampton remained calm and confident throughout, and detectives believed Hampton thought the police actually had nothing on him and were just trying to scare him into confessing. Hampton's DNA was found to match samples taken from the semen that had stained the fly and crotch of Melanie's trousers during that murderous attack. Following his arrest, Hampton released a prepared statement saying: "I deny any involvement in the rape and murder of Melanie Hall."

Meanwhile, forensic scientists continued to work on Hampton's DNA, and further matches were found on four other samples of semen staining Melanie's trousers and pants. Hampton's DNA matched further semen samples taken from Melanie's body during the original post-mortem examination.

It was also found to be present in blood spots located near to where Melanie's body had lain.

On 22 December 2015, Hampton entered a not guilty plea to murder at Bristol Crown Court. Faced with overwhelming forensic evidence, he later changed his plea to guilty and was eventually jailed for life, with a minimum term of 22 years.

There is no doubt that Hampton would never have been caught if it hadn't been for the development of familial DNA, which had led police to his doorstep via his daughter's DNA test. However, DNA and new developments in other forensic technology can't always guarantee bringing criminals to justice.

THE TOUCH

The random reasons for DNA to be found at crime scenes can sometimes mislead cold murder case investigations and send police detectives up the wrong path when it comes to solving a killing.

DAVID BUTLER

In 2011, David Butler, from Liverpool, was arrested at his own home by police and charged with a cold case murder on the basis of what detectives thought was his DNA found at the scene. Mr Butler's DNA sample had been on the UK database since he'd voluntarily given it to the police as part of an investigation into a burglary at his mother's home some years earlier. Mr Butler presumed he could quickly prove he was not the suspect the police were looking for. But detectives were convinced he'd killed a woman called Anne Marie Foy back in 2005, and so began a nightmare for the 65-year-old taxi driver.

Yet Mr Butler's DNA sample had only been a partial match to evidence found at the crime scene. The sample was deemed to be poor quality, and forensic experts warned detectives they couldn't say for sure Mr Butler was guilty, although they were reluctant to completely rule him out as a suspect.

Police insisted they also had CCTV evidence which placed Mr Butler in the area where the murder took place. He ended up spending eight months in prison on murder charges. Merseyside Police convinced the UK's Crown Prosecution Service that there was sufficient evidence for the case to be presented to a jury, and Mr Butler – still pleading his innocence – opted for a jury trial.

Mr Butler's lawyer called a forensic expert to give evidence in court, and this witness explained how a trace of Mr Butler's DNA came to be on the murder victim. Through his work as a taxi driver, Mr Butler's DNA had transferred from his taxi, via money or another person, onto the murder victim. The forensic expert pointed out that the victim had been wearing a glitter nail polish, which proved particularly attractive to dirt – and DNA. It acted almost like a magnet, the court heard. And the police's alleged CCTV "evidence" was also found to be misleading and not admissible. Mr Butler was acquitted on all charges and finally released from prison. The real killer has never been caught and the case remains open.

As one forensic scientist later explained: "Finding DNA proves that a person left a sample. But it doesn't explain how that DNA got there in the first place. The circumstances of a specific crime have to fit that conclusion and that can be the subject of a lot of interpretation." Critics say that, while DNA samples can often be pivotal to a case, each forensic discovery, plus all other evidence, should be dealt with on a case-by-case basis. One criminologist explained: "The scientists were not at fault on the David Butler case. They did their job and found what they thought was his DNA but detectives assumed that match meant Mr Butler had committed the murder, without checking through his own background to find a feasible explanation as to how his DNA came to be at the murder scene." As innocent man David Butler himself later explained: "I think the police have been letting DNA do their job for them and it doesn't. They couldn't even concede they might have got the wrong man."

THE PHANTOM OF HEILBRONN

Law enforcement agents across Europe carried out a 15-year hunt for a suspect after DNA evidence was discovered at the scene of a number of crimes. It was one of the biggest ongoing cold case murder enquiries ever seen on the continent. The suspect even became known in the press as "The Phantom of Heilbronn", after allegedly killing police officer Michèle Kiesewetter in Heilbronn, Germany on 25 April 2007.

A further five murders were eventually attributed to the Phantom of Heilbronn. She was also alternatively referred to as the "Woman Without a Face", because investigators had failed to get even a vague description of her. The existence of this alleged female serial killer had been confirmed via DNA samples found at numerous crime scenes in Austria, France and Germany over most of the first decade of the new century. By March 2009, matching DNA samples had been recovered from a total of 40 crime scenes, ranging from murders to burglaries.

As the case progressed, investigators became increasingly bewildered by the DNA matches because the crime scenes were so far apart. There was a distinct lack of a pattern to the offences as well. The suspect's alleged accomplices seemed to come from a vast range of countries, including Slovakia, Serbia, Romania, Albania and Iraq. Even more mysteriously, the "Phantom of Heilbronn" had never even been caught on any security cameras. Some witnesses to her alleged crimes described her as looking like a man but nothing more precise.

Detectives across Europe insisted they were looking for one offender and confirmed over and over again that their DNA matches made it clear she was female. Over eight years, police forces issued wanted posters and talked in dramatic terms about this notorious female serial killer, who seemed able to disappear into thin air after each crime she committed.

Further extensive DNA tests were then ordered, and scientists working on this now notorious case established that the DNA recovered at all those crime scenes was actually present on the cotton swabs used by all the relevant police forces when they collected DNA samples. It then emerged that the swabs had all been handled by one woman, who worked at the factory where they were manufactured.

Human genetic material had inadvertently been transferred to the forensic sampling equipment, setting off an eight-year hunt for a supposedly dangerous criminal. The cotton swabs at the factory had been put through proper sterilization procedures which were used to kill bacteria, fungi and viruses. They'd been contaminated with human cells in the form of skin particles, sweat, saliva and other bodily secretions from that woman working at the factory.

Police wasted an estimated 2 million euros, as well as more than 16,000 hours of overtime, searching for a female serial killer who didn't exist, and it was all down to the DNA transfer in that factory that made cotton swabs. In addition to the obvious waste of police resources, dozens of often brutal crimes had been committed by offenders who'd never been pursued by police because police investigators were targeting a DNA ghost for those offences. This embarrassing case did at least re-emphasize how easily human-to-product contamination could occur. The introduction of foreign DNA to a crime scene sample – either at the site itself or during laboratory analysis – can lead a criminal investigation up a dead end.

Most members of law enforcement insist that DNA remains the biggest breakthrough in crime detection, despite the "Phantom of Heilbronn" farce and other faulty investigations. Scientists, lawyers and politicians, though, constantly raise new concerns over the quality of forensic evidence. Some have even alleged that most criminal justice systems remain much too reliant on laboratory tests, without appreciating the limitations of such evidence.

THE MISSING

The families of people who disappear for ever don't get the closure they so desperately need. But in recent years, forensic scientists have played an increasingly important role in helping law enforcement investigators with their enquiries, because they are able to extract samples from locations where people have disappeared. This sometimes provides evidence of what has happened to those missing individuals.

One particular case has attracted more attention across the world than any other. This is no doubt because it involves a small child who seemingly disappeared into thin air. In late 2019, one leading American DNA expert announced that he believed he could provide a breakthrough in the case of missing 3-year-old British child Madeleine McCann, who disappeared from a holiday resort in Portugal – if he was allowed to analyze evidence samples taken by UK police officers and forensic scientists. They'd recovered samples when they reinvestigated the case some years after Madeleine's disappearance.

Dr Mark Perlin claimed that the mystery of the little girl's disappearance in 2007 could be solved with the right application of forensic science. Dr Perlin was already well known for running his own Pittsburgh-based Cybernetics team, which had helped identify victims of the 9/11 terror attack. He told one UK newspaper that he wanted to test DNA samples taken from the hotel room where little Madeleine had originally disappeared and the surrounding area. Dr Perlin believed those samples held the key to finding out what had happened to the innocent toddler. He even claimed he could solve the disappearance in just one week *if* he was provided with that DNA evidence.

Other UK-based forensic scientists had already offered their help free of charge to find the missing little girl, but they had not turned up any new evidence. Those UK forensic scientists admitted that unravelling the case was extraordinarily difficult because it was located in another country. There were also unanswered questions about what happened to other exhibits collected by the Portuguese police at the time of the little girl's disappearance. But at the time of writing, there was no sign of the McCanns taking up Dr Perlin's offer. In late 2019, police in Germany announced they were holding a suspect whom they believed was connected to the disappearance of Madeleine McCann.

THE UNSOLVED

It's a rare occurrence, but sometimes even forensic science fails to come up with new breakthrough evidence on cold case investigations. That's when police officers have to go back to basics and reinvestigate every aspect of such a case. "It's important to highlight these cases as well because they show how much of a team effort is needed between police and forensics, especially when it comes to cold cases," explained one former UK murder squad detective. "We can't just refuse to reopen a cold case because there are no forensics to help us."

Surinder Kaur Varyapraj, 36, was last seen alive on 4 February 1996 as she swept snow from the alleyway at the back of her home in Handsworth, Birmingham, England. Neighbours later recalled that they heard a brief high-pitched scream the following morning. A month later Surinder's badly decomposed body was found strangled with a ligature in a bedroom at her home. Nobody was ever arrested for the killing, despite an extensive forensic examination of the scene, including the recovery of an unidentified set of fingerprints.

Twenty-two years later – in December 2018 – detectives in Birmingham reopened the case in the hope that new evidence might help them solve the murder of the mother-of-three. They believed that forensic investigators would be able to recover improved samples of the killer's DNA, thanks to new techniques introduced since the original murder enquiry.

In fact, new DNA samples recovered by forensic experts resulted in a number of earlier suspects being eliminated from police enquiries because their DNA did not match what the investigators believed was the DNA belonging to the killer. And even more troubling, the same DNA samples did not match anyone on the UK's National DNA Database. After this, forensic scientists carried out a familial DNA test, which they logged onto the National DNA Database in order to try and find any close relatives, rather than exact matches. This might then enable detectives to at least track down relatives of the likely killer. But there was no match.

So detectives decided that some good old-fashioned police legwork was needed if they were to stand any chance of cracking the case. Officers mounted a public appeal for new information about a man, who was thought to have lived in the area and had been seen driving a Jaguar XJS at the time of the killing. They publicized the partial registration of the car, which had been mentioned to them by witnesses during the original investigation. Detectives hoped that, as so much time had elapsed since the murder, maybe someone might now feel able to come forward and assist the investigation.

Despite all the efforts of police, forensic scientists and the general public, there was no breakthrough, and the case remains unsolved to this day. As one forensic scientist explained: "Sometimes no amount of science and police work can solve a case. I think a lot of people out there think we will nail the bad guys every time we reopen a cold case. They forget that sometimes you draw a blank. Plain and simple."

THE UNITED STATES
OF CRIME

More cold cases are solved in the US than anywhere else in the world, thanks to a combination of skilful forensic scientists and the nation's extremely high murder rate. It's also reckoned that America's often harsh justice system is riddled with so many holes that often the guilty slip through the system, while the innocent find themselves overwhelmed by it.

The unsolved 1995 murder of prostitute Krystal Lynn Beslanowitch in Utah, in the United States, rested heavily on Detective Todd Bonner's conscience, because he was never able to provide her family with the closure they needed so desperately. Krystal had been 17 years old when she died from a crushing blow to the skull. Her body was found dumped alongside the Provo River.

Krystal had last been seen alive on 15 December 1995, by her boyfriend, when she left their motel in the town of North Temple to get a bite to eat at a nearby convenience store. When she didn't return, the boyfriend called the police. Krystal's body was discovered later that same day on the east bank of the Provo River about five miles north of the town of

Heber by a local rancher. The teenage girl was naked and had severe wounds on her head and shoulders.

Several nearby granite rocks were covered with fresh blood, according to court documents that covered the original murder investigation. The blood on the rocks was considered unrecoverable as far as forensic evidence was concerned. Although Detective Todd Bonner had been outraged by the killing, he had to accept that after months with no concrete leads, the case would have to be filed under unsolved crimes.

Bonner never forgot Krystal Beslanowitch and closely monitored developments in forensic science, always with one eye on persuading his police bosses to reopen the murder probe at some stage. Two full-time detectives were eventually assigned the cold case in 2008, at a time when forensic technology had made significant advances. But all attempts to extract DNA from the blood on the rock that killed Krystal failed.

In 2009, Todd Bonner was elected Wasatch County Sheriff, and he and his colleagues continued to monitor the status of Krystal's case. It wasn't until 2012, though, that scientists were able to use a newly developed forensic vacuum to pick up touch DNA samples from those two bloody rocks that had been used to crush the teenager's skull and kill her.

The vacuum had originally been designed to suck bacteria off food and had been expertly adapted by scientists to collect genetic material left over when someone had been touched or even left saliva on a surface. Touch DNA – also known as trace DNA – is known by these terms because it only requires very small samples of DNA to check in a test. Just the tiniest of skin cells left on an object after it has been touched or casually handled, or even from footprints, is enough to provide a sample.

The touch DNA recovered by forensics from Krystal Beslanowitch's body matched a Joseph Michael Simpson, aged 46, who was on the US national DNA database after serving time in the Utah State Prison in the 1980s for murder. He'd been a resort bus driver in the area where Krystal had been murdered back in 1995 but now resided in Sarasota County, Florida.

The Wasatch County Sheriff's office were advised by prosecutors that they needed stronger DNA evidence to nail the killer. So – with the help of his law enforcement colleagues in Sarasota County – Bonner and another Utah detective tracked down Simpson to his home in Florida, where he was living with his mother, and set up a surveillance operation. The two officers eventually followed Simpson to a shop, where he smoked a cigarette and tossed it aside. Bonner bagged it up and now potentially had extra, up-to-date DNA to test.

A few days later, the sample came out as a complete match to the other DNA recovered from the body of murder victim Krystal. Simpson – by now 46 – was arrested and the following year convicted of murdering Krystal Beslanowitch and sentenced to life in prison.

SARA LYNN WINESKI

Despite new DNA matches, prosecutors in the US often demand further evidence in cold case murder enquiries. This puts forensic scientists and police investigators under immense pressure resulting in a painstaking re-examination of every item of evidence connected to a case, as experts try to unearth the "money shot" that will guarantee that a killer is finally brought to justice.

Transient Sara Lynn Wineski was found strangled and raped in a dark alleyway in St. Petersburg, Florida, in 2005. Nearby residents later said they heard screams at about 11 p.m. that evening. It wasn't until the following afternoon that Sara's body was found under the deck of a nearby building. As a matter of course, DNA evidence was collected by forensic investigators at the scene.

It took two years before a DNA match was found, to a man called Raymond Samuels who was in prison after being sentenced in 2006 to 29 years for robbing and attacking an elderly couple. However, local prosecutors said they weren't comfortable charging Samuels at the time because they felt detectives needed additional evidence to successfully prosecute him.

It wasn't until four years later that further, more sophisticated DNA testing confirmed that Samuels' DNA was not only at the scene, but also on the belt used to strangle Wineski. Around this time, Samuels had also been bragging in prison to other inmates about killing Sara Wineski.

Detectives confirmed that he'd been in the St. Petersburg area for approximately a month at the time of Wineski's murder.

Samuels – also a transient – was extradited to Florida. He was eventually sentenced to life in prison for the murder. Without that DNA match and the skill of the forensic scientists in retrieving it, Samuels' bragging would have been dismissed as "unprovable" and he would probably have never been brought to justice for the murder of Sara Lynn Wineski.

TRIPLE MURDER

Only three decades ago, many cold-blooded killers in the US were getting away with their crimes because of the sheer size of the country. If they had no previous convictions, they were unlikely ever to be caught.

Back in 1990, three prostitutes, Yolanda Sapp, 26, Nickie Lowe, 34, and Kathleen Brisbois, 38, were found dead in Spokane, Washington. They'd all been shot with a .22 calibre handgun, and detectives quickly established through similar evidence at the three crime scenes, plus the method of killing, that they were connected. There was no actual evidence to directly link the crimes to any particular suspect, though. Many men who'd paid the women for sex were reluctant to come forward and help the police, and the investigation fizzled out.

Fifteen years later – in 2005 – the case was reopened by police in the hope that a new forensic examination of the evidence taken at the time of the three murders might provide further DNA and other forensic clues, which it had not been possible to collect at the time of the actual murders all those years earlier. As so often happens with cold case enquiries, it was to be a slow process because the detectives and forensics assigned to the triple murder enquiry were expected to work on current murder cases at the same time. One former forensic scientist explained: "A lot of folk seem to think we drop everything when we take on a cold case. But I'm sorry to say it's just another case to add to our current workload. As a result, it can take one hell of a long time before any new information is actually unearthed."

It wasn't until 2009 – four years later – that forensic investigators managed to recover DNA from the original evidence collected at all three of the murders. This was checked through a federal database, but there were no matches and the case once again ran out of leads.

In 2012, transexual Donna Perry – in her early sixties – was arrested in Washington State on federal charges of possession of illegal firearms. After submitting to a standard DNA test, the sample was found to match that of the DNA connected to the murder of those three women. Other evidence – including old-looking women's panties – were uncovered in a closet in Perry's home. That cupboard contained other items with DNA that proved more forensic links to the murders of the three women.

Perry was arrested and eventually charged with three first-degree murder charges. Her name before a 2000 sex change had been Douglas Perry. In July 2017, a jury in

THE REAL SILENT WITNESSES

Spokane, Washington, convicted Perry, now 65, and she was sentenced to three life terms without the possibility of parole.

PATRICIA BEARD

Law enforcement agencies in many American cities take great pride in reopening cold case murders to try and bring the guilty to justice. Homicide detectives see this as further evidence that police and forensic scientists can work together in unison, and it sends out a message to many of America's on-the-run killers that they will one day be caught.

Mentally disabled Patricia Beard, 32, lived in a one-room apartment in the 500 block of East 11th Avenue, in Denver, Colorado. On 27 March 1981 – after she'd not been seen for several days – a family member went to check on her and found her strangled body in her room. It was a crime without any apparent motive, and Denver police struggled to find any likely suspects. As was so often the case back in those pre-DNA days, the detectives moved on to other investigations when their leads dried up.

Thirty years later – in 2011 – detectives in Denver reopened the forensic crime scene kit on the Patricia Beard case, on the basis that it most likely contained evidence with relevant DNA, which had not been traceable back at the time of the murder but could now be tested for DNA. DNA was eventually recovered and entered into the US's DNA database. It took two more years before a match was flagged up, because the man whose DNA had been recovered didn't submit his

DNA until he was arrested on a minor offence. This positive DNA match to the victim led to murder charges being brought against Hector Bencomo-Hinojos, 53, from Pennsylvania. His wife informed detectives he was a violent man.

Bencomo-Hinojos denied ever knowing Patricia Beard. Yet new DNA evidence clearly proved he'd had sexual contact with her around the time of her death. He was eventually sentenced to 48 years in prison after admitting second-degree murder and second-degree kidnapping in the death of Patricia Beard.

The sentencing of Bencamo-Hinojos was the hundredth rape or murder to be solved by the Denver Cold Case Team.

ANNA PALMER

Re-examining evidence on cold cases can be extremely challenging for forensic scientists. They often have to show great dexterity and patience in order to extract fresh evidence from seemingly impossible scenarios.

Ten-year-old Anna Palmer was attacked and killed in 1998 outside her own front door in Salt Lake City, Utah. The crime was heinous. She'd been stabbed multiple times, but police investigators had no witnesses, little evidence and no apparent suspects.

It wasn't until 11 years later – in 2009 – that forensic analysts were called in to reinvestigate the case. They examined Anna's fingernails for DNA samples using visible and alternative light sources and other equipment not available back at the time of the murder. Forensic scientists eventually found DNA that did not belong to Anna. It was matched on the national DNA database to a man called Matthew Brock, who'd lived just a block away from little Anna at the time of her murder. He was aged 19 at the time of the killing.

Police tracked down Brock to a state prison, where he was serving a 10-year sentence for a sex-related crime with a child. As one detective on the case later explained: "Brock immediately confessed because of that DNA evidence. If we hadn't reopened the case, he would have eventually got out of prison after serving time for those other sex-related offences and probably gone on to murder other innocent children."

In 2011, Brock pleaded guilty to an aggravated murder charge in the death of Anna Palmer and is now serving life in prison.

THE GOLDEN STATE KILLER

There is no doubt that new developments in forensic science, combined with modern technology, have resulted in a dramatic drop in the number of serial killers in countries such as the US and UK over the past two decades. Recent crime databases which track multiple murderers in the Western world over the past century actually show a downward trend in serial murders from the beginning of the 1990s.

Forensic experts and law enforcement agents are convinced that everything from cell phone tracking to computer footprints have helped thwart many potential modern-day serial killers before they even get started. "But we should never forget that some of the most dangerous serial killers of that era are still out there from the 1980s," said one retired Los Angeles homicide detective. "That means we as police investigators are obliged to continue hunting them down and now we have DNA and all the latest forensic science at our disposal to help us."

The Golden State Killer investigation has evolved into the biggest DNA-connected cold case in US criminal history. This unknown serial killer had committed multiple rapes, murders and burglaries across California during a 13-year reign of terror between 1973 and 1986. He'd also been known as the East Area Rapist, Original Night Stalker and the Diamond Knot Killer.

One Californian detective once told me how investigators were so obsessed with catching the Golden State Killer that they'd rush to crime scenes to take a victim's fingerprints using iodine knowing that within a very short time of the death those prints would be much harder to retrieve. "Being able to identify the victim was always the most crucial aspect when it came to investigating a serial killing," explained the same retired officer. "Once we knew who it was, this gave us a chance of tracking that victim's movements, which could lead us to the killer. Without a victim's identity, most murder investigations back then had little chance of being solved."

Despite a vast state-wide manhunt during the 1980s, the Golden State Killer completely disappeared off the crime scene radar in 1986 following his last known attack. Throughout his murderous reign, detectives had meticulously collected samples of blood, saliva, fingerprints and semen linked to his crimes, but they'd never been able to match anyone on the FBI's national DNA database.

In 2016, the cold case enquiry into the unsolved Golden State Killer crimes was officially reopened, although few believed it stood much chance of bringing this most feared of all US serial killers to justice. In fact, so much time had elapsed since the last of the killer's known crimes was committed in 1986 that most detectives believed he'd probably died since then. This theory was further backed up by the lack of DNA matches from the samples taken from the original evidence of the killings, even using the familial DNA system.

Forensic scientists then recommended using the familial DNA system in a different way from before. This time the samples from the crime scenes were uploaded to a genealogy website called GED Match instead of the US national DNA database. The sample immediately matched several relatives of the killer. That list was narrowed down using information such as the suspected killer's location and age, which had been estimated by FBI profilers after he'd committed each murder more than 30 years earlier.

This painstaking process eventually led detectives to former police officer Joseph James DeAngelo, now in his seventies. He lived in a suburb of Sacramento, California, that was close to the scene of the first few murders more than 40 years earlier. Investigators managed to collect a much more substantial DNA sample from his discarded trash while they had him under surveillance.

DeAngelo was arrested at his home. Hours later, he was left alone in an interrogation room. Detectives watched on CCTV with bemusement as he began speaking to himself, seeming to address a person within that he could not control. "I did all that," DeAngelo said to his "other self". "I didn't have the strength to push him out. He made me. He went with me. It was like in my head, I mean, he's a part of me. I didn't want to do those things. I pushed Jerry out and had a happy life. I did all those things. I destroyed all their lives. So now I've got to pay the price." Prosecutors later expressed scepticism over whether DeAngelo's words and actions were authentic, noting he once faked a heart attack after being caught shoplifting.

In June 2020, DeAngelo admitted to a total of 13 murders in a deal with US prosecutors which was meant to spare him the death penalty. He also admitted to numerous rapes, burglaries and other crimes. He currently remains in isolation in a Sacramento jail awaiting trial.

Detectives who finally apprehended DeAngelo know he would never have been brought to justice if they hadn't submitted those DNA samples onto the genealogy site. Detectives in the US and UK remain confident that it's only a matter of time before further serial killers out there are brought to justice, no matter how long ago they committed their crimes.

KAREN KLAAS

Cold case murder investigators constantly refer to the expertise of forensic scientists and how their latest, highly sensitive equipment can now trace any DNA – however small an amount – if there is some to be found. "These scientists have helped put away a lot of bad people in recent years," explained one Los Angeles homicide detective. "No police officer wants to have an unsolved murder on his conscience, however many years earlier that killing was committed. That's why most of us try never to forget about the victims."

Karen Klaas, aged 32, was raped and strangled with her own tights in her Hermosa Beach, California, home on 30 January 1976. She was the ex-wife of Righteous Brothers pop singer Bill Medley. On that same day, Karen had been due to meet two friends and neighbours for coffee after having taken her young son to school in Manhattan Beach. When she did not turn up, one of her friends went to her home and noticed a white man with bushy, curly brown hair leaving the house. Moments later, Karen was found by her friend and rushed to hospital where she remained in a coma for five days before dying on 4 February 1976.

A mountain of publicity followed the murder thanks to her former husband's fame. Wild rumours circulated about who the most likely suspects were for the killing, but they all proved to be the figment of people's imagination, twisted by their fascination with the murder of a celebrity's ex-wife. The police eventually ran out of leads and shelved the case.

In 1999, detectives revived the investigation thanks to DNA technology, which had not existed at the time of the murder. Fortunately, police had collected multiple biological samples from the scene during the original investigation, which could now be tested for DNA. Those samples ruled out five of the original suspects for the killing because they did not match the DNA recovered from that evidence. This left police no nearer to finding the actual perpetrator, and the investigation once again ran out of leads and was put back into the Hermosa Beach police department's cold case file.

In 2015, forensic scientists were approached by cold case detectives in Hermosa Beach who wanted to trace relatives of the unknown killer by putting his DNA samples into the familial DNA system and seeing what names came up in the national database. The familial DNA test matched a man with a criminal record for a number of extremely violent crimes. Detectives immediately presumed they'd found their man without needing to go through an entire family tree. But they had to then discount that suspect because his DNA was not a complete match to the samples taken from the original murder scene.

Lead detectives switched their attention to another family member who seemed to fit the bill. His name was Kenneth Troyer. Troyer – 29 at the time of the Karen Klass murder – had been shot and killed in March 1982, while escaping from California Men's Colony State Prison, in San Obispo. Troyer was suspected of involvement in numerous other robberies, assaults and rapes in Orange County, near to where Karen Klass had been slain.

Establishing that Troyer had been Karen's murderer after a 40-year gap did at least give her family some closure. Ex-husband Bill Medley later told reporters he'd always hoped

Karen's case would be solved. "It's closure," Medley said in 2017. "When I was told, I just kind of became numb because this is something you've been hoping for – speculating about for 40 years – and all of sudden they say 'we got him' and here's who did it." He added, "We miss Karen and the most important thing is the boys didn't get to grow up with their mother. She would have been an incredible grandma and she was a wonderful, wonderful girl. My ex-wife was one of my best friends after the divorce."

BUNGLING DNA LABORATORIES

DNA is just as susceptible to being used corruptly or inefficiently as any other type of forensic evidence. In the US, this has led to miscarriages of justice on an almost industrial scale.

THE HOUSTON POLICE DEPARTMENT CRIME LABORATORY

In Houston, Texas, a clever bit of work by journalists in 2002 helped uncover an outrageous DNA forensics scandal, which would never have been exposed if it hadn't been for their tenacious investigation. The Houston Police Department Crime Laboratory – one of the largest public forensic centres in the state – handled DNA evidence from at least 500 cases every year. These were mostly rapes and murders, but occasionally burglaries and armed robberies. Acting on a tip from a whistle-blower, a local TV station obtained dozens of DNA profiles processed by that laboratory and sent them to independent experts for re-analysis. The results were stunning: Houston police technicians had regularly completely misinterpreted even the most basic of samples.

In one case in 1998, a teenager had been falsely accused of rape after a DNA sample had been wrongly classified as coming from him. The boy and his friend, also accused of rape, had given complete alibis to police, but the DNA said they were guilty. Yet the two teenagers didn't even fit the descriptions of the attackers. They were sentenced to 25 years each in prison. And it wasn't until the journalistic exposure of the Houston crime laboratory that their relatives realized there was a chance to overturn this gross miscarriage of justice.

New examinations of the teenagers' DNA showed that the profiles did not fit as a perfect match, which is supposed to be the requisite for any case. Instead, the technician who examined the original sample had made an incorrect judgement, and it had cost two teenagers their liberty and changed their entire lives. Technicians from the same Houston crime lab had wrongly stated that all the semen found in the car where the woman had been raped belonged to those two teenage boys. They were eventually released from prison more than four years after their original arrest.

Not long after they left jail, a cold hit in the FBI's Combined DNA Index System led police to a convicted felon called Donnie Lamon Young. Young confessed that he and an accomplice had raped that Houston woman in her car back in 1998. Young eventually pleaded guilty to the crime and was given a lengthy prison sentence.

THE LAS VEGAS METROPOLITAN
POLICE DEPARTMENT CRIME LAB

But there wasn't just one "rogue" forensic laboratory making human errors in the United States. On 6 November 2001, a Las Vegas woman and her two young daughters were attacked in their home by a man in a mask holding a baseball bat. The invader demanded money. The woman had just $23 in her wallet, so the assailant found the woman's bank card, forced her and her two daughters into their car and made her drive to an ATM machine to withdraw more cash. After a number of attempts when the card wouldn't work, they headed back towards the house. Meanwhile, back at the family's empty home, the victim's husband had returned with their son and immediately deduced that something was wrong. He immediately left the house in his car to search for his wife and daughters. He quickly spotted his wife's car and approached the vehicle. The man fled with the baseball bat he'd been carrying throughout the incident.

The woman described the intruder as a black youth wearing a ski mask and a dark blue hooded sweatshirt. Police later canvassed the area and eventually spotted 18-year-old Dwayne Jackson riding his bike with his cousin, Howard Grissom. Despite both matching only the most basic description of the intruder as being black, police followed them as they entered a house. The officers looked into a car parked on the driveway of the same house. Inside the vehicle, they claimed they saw a dark blue hooded sweatshirt with a black ski mask in the pocket. It matched the description given out by police.

Minutes later, police raided the house, and the two teenagers Jackson and Grissom were arrested. Each provided DNA samples, taken by the Las Vegas Metro Police Department crime lab. They found that Jackson's DNA matched the sample taken from the sweatshirt originally seen in the car outside the house, and he was charged with burglary, robbery and three counts of kidnapping. His cousin was never arrested because there was no DNA evidence against him. The victim and her husband failed to identify Jackson at a subsequent identity parade. The DNA "match" was the only evidence connecting Jackson to the crime.

Warned by his lawyer that he faced a life sentence if convicted, Jackson pleaded guilty to one count of robbery in exchange for dropping the burglary and kidnapping charges. He was sentenced to four years in prison in January 2003 and eventually released on parole in late 2006.

In November 2010, the California Justice Department contacted the Las Vegas Metro PD and informed them that someone else in their system had matched the DNA from the evidence that had resulted in Jackson spending years in jail. That DNA had come from Jackson's cousin Grissom, who'd been with Jackson on the day of the raid on that house. Years after that home invasion in Las Vegas, Grissom had been convicted of manslaughter in California and provided authorities with his DNA. This had been uploaded onto the US DNA database and produced a hit on that earlier kidnap and robbery.

Over the following seven months, police re-examined the case and checked DNA evidence again to confirm the error. It eventually emerged that the laboratory technician in Las Vegas had accidentally switched Jackson's and Grissom's DNA samples in the lab before testing during the original investigation.

In April 2011, the Metro police department informed Jackson of the mix-up and he was fully exonerated and cleared of all involvement in the robbery kidnapping. As a result of that DNA mix-up, Dwayne Jackson had spent nearly four years in Nevada prisons for a crime he did not commit. The miscarriage of justice which led to Jackson's imprisonment sparked a re-examination of at least two hundred cases handled by the same lab technician. A number of cases were eventually invalidated because of incorrect and faulty testing.

THE MADRID BOMBING MIX-UP

In the US today, lawmakers demand much more scrutiny of forensic evidence and the working practices of scientists, technicians and laboratories throughout the country. But back in 2004, forensic evidence was rarely challenged, and many believe that this led to one of the most outrageous miscarriages of justice ever seen in the United States.

In May that year, lawyer Brandon Mayfield was arrested in Portland, Oregon, on a material witness warrant, less than two months after the Madrid terrorist bombings in Spain, which killed 191 people and wounded more than 1,800.

According to an FBI affidavit at the time, Mr Mayfield's fingerprint was identified as being on a blue plastic bag containing detonators found in a van used by the bombers. An FBI fingerprint analysist identified "in excess of 15 points of identification during his comparison" and the FBI announced they had a "100 percent" match to that fingerprint, and Mr Mayfield was arrested.

In fact, the FBI crime lab handling Mr Mayfield's DNA sample had been over-worked and took unnecessary shortcuts. They'd mixed up the forensic evidence and ended up processing a fingerprint sent from police in Spain on another case, rather than the alleged suspect's print. Mr Mayfield was released several days later, and later claimed he'd also been a victim of profiling because he was a Muslim convert.

It was only after the FBI reviewed testimony by its forensic comparison analysts that it admitted finding possible errors in at least 90 per cent of similar cases. Many presumed this case was just the tip of the iceberg. The American National Academy of Sciences conceded that there were serious problems with the standard of work performed by many crime laboratories across the United States. ANAS stated: "Amongst existing forensic practices only DNA analysis has been rigorously shown to be consistent. Everything from finger printing to firearms identification needs to be improved." Besides these facilities being overworked, it was claimed that there were not enough certification programmes for investigators and technicians, and that the entire field had not been properly developed.

The US Justice Department eventually had to pay out $2 million and apologized to Mr Mayfield for wrongly accusing him of being a terrorist. That written apology read: "The United States of America apologizes to Mr. Brandon Mayfield and his family for the suffering caused by the FBI's misidentification of Mr. Mayfield's fingerprint and the resulting investigation of Mr. Mayfield, including his arrest as a material witness in connection with the 2004 Madrid train bombings and the execution of search warrants and other court orders in the Mayfield family home and in Mr. Mayfield's law office." The US Justice Department later insisted the FBI had taken steps to improve its fingerprint identification process "to ensure that what happened does not happen again."

It's claimed that collection and testing standards for DNA and other crime scene evidence have greatly improved in the US since many of the cases outlined in this book occurred. Crime laboratories in the US insist they're much more thorough and disciplined with their testing techniques and that the training of staff is more intense than it used to be. One Californian forensic scientist explained: "Today it's drilled into the laboratory analysts and forensic scientists that they must guard against contamination at all times and extraction techniques have been greatly refined in recent years as a result, but there is always room for error."

The Innocence Project in the United States – which has exposed miscarriages of justice since 1992 – continues to highlight faults in forensic testing systems. They claim these problems are often driven by racism and prejudice endemic to the US criminal justice system. The Innocence Project has won almost two hundred exonerations of trials related to the use of DNA testing alone. In the majority of the cases, the wrongfully convicted were black.

EXPERT'S EVIDENCE

Forensic evidence hinges on the word of its scientists, and the interpretation of their work can sometimes wrongly influence a judge and jury during a murder trial. Most scientists insist that the blame for this lies at the feet of the people – the police and lawmakers involved in the justice system – and has nothing to do with the actual results of their evidence gathering.

"Forensic science needs to remain scientific," explained one forensic expert. "It should be taken as such. We don't have the right to give opinions, which can cost citizens their freedom. We just present the facts. Our findings should speak for us and this constant need to interpret the science to suit the case at hand in court cases is wrong. The stakes are very high when you're using forensic science in court to convict people and *nothing* is ever set in stone." The same scientist added: "Our information can be twisted to fit a case and that shouldn't happen. It's put us all in the firing line, which is wrong."

In the US, the misinterpretation of the testimony of forensic scientists has led to some gross miscarriages of justice, which resulted in dozens of people being jailed for crimes they did not commit.

DENTAL TWIST

US courts regularly use forensic odontologists to testify in criminal trials, despite a lack of tangible scientific proof that a suspect's teeth can be identified from a bite mark on a victim's skin. More than two decades ago, the US's National Academy of Science issued a dire warning in a report entitled "Strengthening Forensic Science in the United States: A Path Forward". It stated there was "no scientific basis for identifying an individual [through bite mark comparison] to the exclusion of all others". Yet under oath, six forensic dental experts helped convince a jury in 1982 that the marks found on a murder victim belonged to one particular man. As a result, alleged killer Keith Harward, from Virginia, was found guilty of murder at his trial and sentenced to life in prison.

Harward was alleged to have broken into the home of a couple, killing a man and raping his wife. During the course of the attack, Harward was alleged to have bitten the wife's legs repeatedly. The wife – who was never able to positively identify Mr Harward as the man who attacked her – told police that her attacker was wearing a sailor's uniform. During the early stages of the murder investigation, a dentist reviewed the dental records of marines stationed at the nearby naval base and initially excluded Keith Harward.

But six months later, Harward became a prime suspect after his then-girlfriend reported to police that he'd bitten her during a dispute. Further forensic dentistry tests convinced detectives they had the right man. At Harward's eventual trial, the six bite mark analysts agreed that marks found on the victim matched Harward's teeth, and his fate was sealed.

In April 2016 – after more than 30 years of proclaiming his innocence from his prison cell – Harward, now 60, was allowed to submit a DNA sample to be compared with DNA recovered from the original murder scene. This proved Harward was not the killer rapist after all. Instead, the DNA profile matched a criminal called Jerry Crotty – who'd died in an Ohio prison in 2006. Crotty had provided law enforcement with a DNA sample after a 2002 conviction for abduction. Crotty and Harward had been in the Navy together at the time of the original murder and rape. Virginia's Supreme Court proclaimed that Harward was an innocent man.

Harward's case highlighted the weaknesses of forensic testimony when it was directly used to help convict people of crimes. One forensic scientist later explained: "Teeth, hair, fibre, tool marks, firearms and ballistics, even voice comparisons are not always correct, even though they're often presented as such in court by prosecutors. In Mr Harward's case, multiple forensic dental experts presented their opinions to a jury, which resulted in a wrongful imprisonment. That tells you everything about what an inexact science we are part of."

Keith Harward was released from Nottaway Correctional Center in Burkeville, Virginia, in April 2016 after 33 years in prison. It's believed he was at least the twenty-fifth person in the US to have been wrongfully convicted or indicted on murder charges because of bite mark evidence.

THE
SILENT
WITNESS
STORY

Don't you understand that feeling, it's obsessive.
I'm sorry, I really am. You find something, you want
the answers, PDQ, you just have to have them.

SILENT WITNESS FORENSIC SCIENTIST NIKKI ALEXANDER

A PROGRAMME IS BORN

In the mid-1990s, drug-related violence meant that homicide figures were rising fast in the UK, US and many other nations in the Western world. The narcotics marketplace was highly lucrative, and rival gangs were engaged in indiscriminate, bloody turf wars that often cost innocent bystanders their lives. In order to improve arrest figures at that time, senior officers and Home Office bosses in the UK started putting enormous pressure on police officers and scientists, in particular. Politicians demanded improvements in law and order, and large sums of public money were being spent on forensic science laboratories.

Following the introduction of DNA fingerprinting and other new forensic science developments, police detectives and the experts alongside them believed they were about to turn a corner and be able to solve cases they would have walked away from in previous times. As a result, the status of forensic scientists was rising to the point where they were being recognized as legitimate investigators. Some of these experts coming through the ranks were fast gaining reputations as clever investigators in their own right.

However, this also meant that forensic scientists began being put under enormous pressure by police forces across the UK to come up with results. Many detectives unashamedly leaned on them to solve some of the toughest cases. "It started to get very tricky," one former Scotland Yard murder squad detective from that era recalled. "A lot of my police colleagues got a bit lazy and put all the pressure onto the forensic boys to solve many of the most serious crimes, especially murder."

And watching all this at the time was a young former police officer turned BBC scriptwriter called Nigel McCrery. He'd quit the force to study Modern History at Cambridge, before entering a BBC graduate training scheme. During his time as a constable, McCrery had seen more than his fair share of bodies and even attended post-mortems. In the mid-1990s, he worked on programmes such as *Crime Limited* and *Tomorrow's World*, before becoming a researcher on the TV drama *Our Friends in the North*.

McCrery could see that the relationship between the police and forensic scientists had become much more complex since he'd quit Nottinghamshire Police a few years earlier. He recognized that this might make good television drama, and he knew the BBC were looking for a new police series. So it was in this exciting new law enforcement era of the mid-1990s that Nigel McCrery began to map out his programme idea that centred around a team of expert forensic scientists.

The creation of any TV drama is a complex business. It's not just a matter of writing an outline with a few pages on it. The process is lengthy and usually involves a pilot script and something called "A Bible", which outlines many of the future episodes, all the main characters and how the programme will develop from a dramatic point of view. In the end, McCrery's bosses at the BBC were impressed by his highly original creation, which he called *Silent Witness*. The programme was commissioned relatively quickly, because the corporation wanted a reasonably fast turnaround on a crime series that they could air speedily.

Silent Witness was first screened in 1996. The main character was a gritty, no-nonsense pathologist called Sam Ryan, played by actress Amanda Burton. The series even came with its own unique format. Instead of self-contained episodes, each story would consist of two episodes. The first nine series typically featured eight episodes (four two-part stories), and this increased to ten episodes (five two-part stories) from the tenth series onwards. The approach of the programme was unique from the start. It didn't dwell on the crimes themselves or the plodding police officers trying their hardest to bring the bad guys and girls to justice. It led with the science.

KEY TO SUCCESS

Today, most of those involved with the current production of *Silent Witness* fully expect the TV drama to continue being one of the world's longest-running TV series for many years to come. One of the keys to that success is that *Silent Witness* is constantly looking for fresh ideas and new, original plot-lines, while at the same time serving up some serious drama, as well as the obligatory explosions, drugs and death.

Ever since its launch, the series has been praised for its determination to accurately reflect forensic science and the role of its experts in helping to bring criminals to justice. From pre-production on *Silent Witness*'s very first episode back in 1996, right up to today's version, the series has always had at least one respected forensic advisor on set to make sure the series achieves that finely balanced line between reality and good drama.

The forensic consultants attached to every series of *Silent Witness* since its launch all those years ago operate in conjunction with the show's director, producers, writers and cast to ensure that the series achieves an air of authority. To many in the forensic profession, these programme consultants are the unsung heroes who make sure that forensic science is fairly and accurately portrayed in *Silent Witness*. Most agree they have achieved that in most instances.

It's not been an easy balancing act for the technical advisors, though. One source inside *Silent Witness* told me that its team of writers often use the show's forensic consultant for reference material, so that an episode can be rounded off with an unusual type of death, because perfect cliff-edge endings remain the prerequisite for all good TV drama. As one former producer of the show explained:

> It's all about suspending disbelief when it comes to good drama. You have to believe in the characters and the plausibility of the plotlines. That's why the forensic consultant is such an important part of the programme. But you also have to allow a drama to take you on a ride into a world that may not really exist. *Silent Witness* doesn't want to overplay the technical side of forensic science but at the same time the viewers must believe the show's characters know what they're talking about.

The same veteran BBC producer added: "You can't get everything absolutely accurate because that might mean sacrificing good drama, which is ultimately what the audience expects. But it's vital to convince the viewers that this is as real as any drama can be."

The time at which *Silent Witness* was devised perfectly mirrors the evolution of the world of forensic science up to today. This may well be one of the pivotal contributory factors when it comes to actually putting your finger on why *Silent Witness* has proved so successful. But no doubt when former policeman Nigel McCrery created the series back in 1996, he could not have envisaged the direction of the show, as well as its extraordinary longevity.

By charting the development of forensic science in the years since *Silent Witness* first hit the small screen, this book has tried to provide a comprehensive insight into both the real and fictional worlds.

GOODBYE SAM RYAN

Back in 2004, actress Amanda Burton – who played the original lead pathologist Sam Ryan – took the *Silent Witness* producers by surprise and decided to quit. She'd featured in the first seven series following its launch in 1996. One BBC insider claimed at the time: "Amanda definitely knows her own mind. Her departure is a blow to the BBC and puts the future of *Silent Witness* in doubt." At first, there were rumours that the series would be shelved because its main star was no longer on board. But like all well-established entities – whether it be a football team or a TV drama series – the management of *Silent Witness* was never going to let it perish just because one person had decided to jump ship.

A decision was made following Amanda Burton's departure in 2004 to change the direction of the series and take it more upmarket by recruiting actress Emilia Fox as star pathologist Nikki Alexander. She came from the Fox acting dynasty, and was about as far removed from the blunt, plain-speaking character Sam Ryan as you can get. Emilia Fox immediately fitted into her role almost seamlessly, and within weeks of her debut as lead pathologist Nikki Alexander, fans of the show were voicing their approval of her character, and appeals for the return of her predecessor Sam Ryan soon faded out. Since then, Emilia Fox's character Nikki has gone from strength to strength, thanks to a combination of vulnerability and toughness when it comes to the way she leads her life as a sometimes lonely middle-aged lady.

A lot of the show's female fans who've tuned into the series since Nikki's introduction believe they have a connection with *Silent Witness* because Nikki goes through so many classic domestic problems during the course of the show. Some viewers even openly admit that *Silent Witness*'s pivotal dramatic content that revolves around dead bodies is nothing more than a side issue compared to following glamorous Nikki's domestic and professional life, with all its complicated twists and turns. One ardent fan of *Silent Witness* explained: "The series has managed to weave everyday storylines into the main thrust of each episode to guarantee that no matter how technical the forensic details are, the everyday pressures of life are not ignored. It's clever because it means one doesn't really consider the series to be a procedural drama, although at the end of the day it is very much that."

Emilia Fox's character Nikki sums up the issues between her personal and professional life when she says in one episode: "One day I'll end up stiff and cold like some badly wigged mannequin in a scary local museum. Someone will show me as an exhibit. 'This is Dr Alexander, our 92-year-old pathologist. Remarkably, Dr Alexander is now completely desiccated apart from the tiny muscles which operate her rusty scalpel.'" As the same fan of the show pointed out:

"That's a brilliant bit of dialogue because Nikki sums up her attitude and fears that she'll one day end up on life's scrapheap unloved and uncared for having failed to find domestic happiness, despite some extraordinary achievements as a forensic investigator.

Nikki Alexander and her team's approach to each case in *Silent Witness* is obviously crucial to the success of the series. She is a highly innovative pathologist, whose expertise in archaeology and forensic anthropology makes her an invaluable asset. But the producers of the series like to keep the audience guessing. As one former executive on the series explained: "No one is guaranteed their place on the show so it's impossible to know what characters will survive in future series."

THE REAL
NIKKI ALEXANDER

These days there are many more female forensic scientists in the UK than there were when *Silent Witness* debuted in 1996. The series' original head pathologist Sam Ryan was said to have been loosely based on a forensic pathologist whom series creator Nigel McCrery had worked with during his days as a policeman in Nottingham. She was an up-and-coming young scientist based in Sheffield when *Silent Witness* first launched. Today, other supposed inspirations have emerged, who have no doubt influenced the characteristics of Dr Nikki Alexander. One of those inspirations is Professor Angela Gallop.

Gallop grew up in Oxford in an academic household but actually only just managed to get enough O levels to stay at school. She eventually ended up at Sheffield University studying botany and plant science. Gallop began her career as an academic examining sea slugs. Then she saw an advert for a job in the Forensic Science Service and the rest was, as they say, history.

Like so many forensic investigators, Professor Gallop has never forgotten her first corpse. It was a bitterly cold Friday night in February 1978. She had been working for the FSS for three years, but she'd never before seen the victim of a violent killing. The body was that of an 18-year-old prostitute called Helen Rytka. She'd been hit five times over the head with a hammer and repeatedly stabbed in the chest. She also happened to be the eighth of thirteen women to die at the hands of Peter Sutcliffe, the notorious Yorkshire Ripper. Like so many other of her colleagues, Professor Gallop was struck by the way this teenage girl looked so peaceful, and later noted that this is so often the case with the victims of violent crime. One of the few killers Professor Gallop actually came face to face with was ripper Peter Sutcliffe. She later explained: "I remember seeing Peter Sutcliffe and thinking how inoffensive he looked. Evil can come with many faces."

Professor Gallop has worked on some of the UK's most notorious killings of the past 40 years, ranging from correcting serious miscarriages of justice to many challenging murder cases. In 2003, she uncovered critical evidence in the trial of a man called Jeffrey Gafoor, who was accused of the 1988 murder of a 20-year-old prostitute called Lynette White. Her forensic evidence helped three men from Cardiff – known as "The Cardiff Three" – get their convictions overturned after they'd been framed for the murder by crooked policemen.

On the surface, Gallop comes across as a thorough, detached professional. But underneath it – just like her TV counterpart Nikki Alexander – there are occasions when she cannot help taking her work home with her. Gallop admitted to a journalist once that her job had a profound effect on her psyche. She said that while walking on her own in the countryside, she often thinks about dead bodies and the places that could be the perfect locations to dump them. Typically, she's more concerned with the effect these types of issues have on her colleagues inside the forensic world and has even been instrumental in trying to introduce counselling for any forensic scientists who felt impacted by their work.

Gallop also admitted in another interview that the intensity of her job has led to a serious inability to manage small talk in most circumstances. She explained: "If someone asks what I think about something I can't make an unqualified statement, even about a cake I'm about to eat. It's exhausting. To relax, I love the drama of opera. I know it's mad, but then life is mad."

Professor Gallop is also renowned for her skills at reconstructing crime scenes, which have been praised by many inside the closely knit UK forensic science community. These reconstructions can involve everything from dripping blood into a telephone to work out how an injured person interacted with it, to shooting a suspended pig carcass with a shotgun to ascertain where the shot went.

Professor Gallop is still passionate about her work and open about the motives that drive her. "It is justice, it is fairness," she told one reporter recently. "My mum was a great one for fairness and saying you have got to be nice to people. I think it comes from that. The power of science is just incredible, it is amazing what we can do for people."

THE *SILENT WITNESS* "JUGGERNAUT"

Until very recently, *Silent Witness*'s team of forensic scientists consisted of Nikki Alexander (Emilia Fox), Jack Hodgson (David Caves) and Clarissa Mullery (Liz Carr), backed up by overall boss Tom Chamberlain (Richard Lintern). These characters drove forward the series' storylines, which included such emotive subjects as drugs, violence against trans people and flaws within the justice system, as well as corrupt police officers.

No wonder *Silent Witness* is today considered a drama juggernaut inside the BBC. One TV industry insider explained: "No executive at the BBC would want to be known as the person who axed *Silent Witness*. I'm not saying that is keeping the show going. Far from it, *Silent Witness* is there on its own merit but it has built for itself an immensely strong power base."

Every week during *Silent Witness*'s pre-production process – long before the filming of an actual episode begins – executives and writers hold regular conferences to kick around new ideas, and it's made clear during these meetings that the series can cover any subject it wants. But rest assured, if it ever crosses the line into being far-fetched, then *Silent Witness*'s fans soon come down on the show like the proverbial ton of bricks.

ACCURACY AND
AUTHENTICITY

The forensic scientists on *Silent Witness* are capable of solving a wide variety of clever, intricate crimes. While never rehashing actual true crime stories, the show still manages to provide its audience with a convincingly authentic window into the world of forensic medicine. Many believe this is partly because the writers of *Silent Witness* have always been given the freedom to come up with fast-moving, original plotlines.

Some critics, however, have accused *Silent Witness* of sometimes giving the impression forensic investigations revolve around hunches, rather than solid, old-fashioned, scientific facts and figures. How many times have we seen that knowing look on current Lyell team leader Nikki Alexander's face when she realizes the significance of some random event she's noticed that we, the audience, wouldn't have thought twice about? As one former BBC producer explained: "That's television for you. It's all about making the drama work. Why should accuracy be allowed to get in the way of a good story?"

Some audience members have been highly critical in recent years about the flashy, arty, over-designed look of the laboratory at the Lyell Centre, where Nikki Alexander and her team work and spend much of each episode. Many forensic scientists I've spoken to say real-life versions of such laboratories usually have working conditions which are more akin to Victorian times. One ardent fan of the show – who happens to be a forensic scientist – told me:

> There never seems to be an instrument out of place in the Lyell Centre and that does sometimes grate with me. It's just not like that in real life. The producers need to be careful because if they make the Lyell centre too perfect and sterile, then it might start to detract from all the hard work its scientists are involved with. Instead of surfaces that you could eat your dinner off they should spread a bit of blood and gore around and leave a few old sandwiches and overfull bins around the place. A lot of my colleagues feel the same way as me about this.

Actress Emilia Fox has undoubtedly worked hard to ensure her character Nikki Alexander appeals to a wide demographic, although there are moments when she seems somewhat overdressed while performing some particularly grisly post-mortems. As one practising forensic scientist said:

> It does stretch the whole thing a bit to see Nikki dressed to the nines as she cuts open a skull and removes a dead man's brain. But on the other hand, I have to say the way she does it is actually fairly accu-

ACCURACY AND AUTHENTICITY

rate. She peels back the skin, as one would do, and removes the brain mass in one large chunk. On *Silent Witness* you often see organs taken out individually, although it has to be said that us mere mortals in the real world do tend to remove them all from the torso in one session. But I'll give them that one because no doubt the programme makers want to ensure they achieve the maximum shock factor from each scene in the lab, otherwise it might get a bit boring.

In 2011, dozens of viewers complained about a scene that began with Nikki Alexander becoming distressed as she performed an autopsy on an eight-year-old girl, who'd been brutally raped and murdered. "Never look into their eyes," she says in the middle of her examination. That comment sparked dozens of angry remarks, and one viewer commented on social media: "This programme bears about as much resemblance to reality as a badger does to a stealth bomber." One forensic scientist commented after seeing the episode: "It was a mistake for her to say that because we have to remain detached at all times during an autopsy, otherwise we wouldn't be able to do our job properly. It's all very well Nikki having a heart and soul but being professional is a number one priority, during even the most difficult moments. In any case, how can you properly perform an autopsy if you don't look directly at all parts of a corpse."

Others in the world of forensic science believe that *Silent Witness* needs to spend more time *inside* the Lyell

Centre laboratories and offices than even the latest version of the show does. "Sometimes it seems as if the scientists are beating the police to the scene of actual crimes and it's never like that in real life," said one recently retired London murder squad detective.

Other police officers say that scenes featuring forensic scientists sitting in on actual interviews of suspects are "somewhat far-fetched". One former detective explained: "There is no way I'd allow a boffin to sit in on an interview I was conducting with a criminal. I'm extremely relieved to see that *Silent Witness* has cut back on doing that in the more recent episodes. But the makers need to be careful not to allow it to creep back in."

One former murder detective told me: "The scientists don't always appreciate they need us just as much as we need them and that needs to continue to be carefully portrayed in the series. "After all, we're still the ones who at the end of the day have to add two and two together to get the actual results. We are the ones who have to go right into the firing line, regardless of the danger. Although you don't always get that impression from *Silent Witness*."

Some of today's criminals claim that *Silent Witness* itself gives the impression that forensic investigators are godlike figures who're never wrong. One former bank robber told me: "The way they make it look on *Silent Witness* there is virtually no point in being a criminal because you'll never get away with anything. But that's not always the case. Those forensic scientists may be clever when it comes to test tubes and DNA swabs but they're not out on the streets literally catching the villains. I reckon there are still opportunities out there for good operators who know how to spot an opportunity."

While some forensic scientists I've spoken to have questioned the authenticity of *Silent Witness*, none have criticized its unique ability to ensure that studying the dead appeals to such a wide cross-section of the viewing public. *Silent Witness*'s producers have even recently scaled back the Lyell staff's close involvement with the police during investigations. Today's episodes have gone out of their way to emphasize a clear line between the scientists and the police. As one BBC insider explained: "This is important because forensic scientists do not want to be accused of being too friendly with the police. They want their independence, so they can make informed unbiased decisions when it comes to the crimes they're investigating." Most of these recent structural changes to *Silent Witness* have been extremely subtle, though. Producers describe it as a "gentle drip feed" of changes, and there's no doubt it has helped to keep the series feeling fresh and innovative.

But one particular scene, in an episode of *Silent Witness* in January 2018, provoked a furious backlash. Viewers were left bewildered by a bizarre blunder in which pathologist Nikki found herself trapped in a bathroom after a steamy night of passion with her new American boyfriend, Matt. She could hear an altercation outside but couldn't get the door to open. Then suddenly the latch came free and she was able to pull the door open and a chair that had been lodged underneath the doorknob fell to the floor as if by magic.

Baffled by the scene, many *Silent Witness* viewers took to Twitter to debate this allegedly "unrealistic" piece of drama. "I'm not sure the chair would have stopped the door from opening?" one viewer questioned. Another slammed: "Why put a chair against a door that opens inwards?" One audience member complained: "Oh well. So much for Matt. So much for bigger holes than usual in the plot." Another fan added: "Absolute rubbish!! You can't wedge a door closed from the outside if it opens inward."

The BBC and the series' producers never publicly commented on all this, but it was a timely reminder that audiences expect realism throughout *Silent Witness* and that they will always be there to spot the blemishes. However, one fan later put an interesting spin on this by saying: "All those moans and groans show just how much the show means to so many people. I think it's healthy to get a reaction, even a negative one like that. It shows people care and it's a gentle warning to the show's producers not to ever let the show's high standards slip."

So there's no denying that *Silent Witness* can sometimes overstretch reality and end up taking its own credibility to the limit. But considering there have been 140 plus episodes of *Silent Witness* since its launch in 1996, there have been relatively few duff scenes.

SILENT WITNESS
AND LONDON

Getting *Silent Witness* to "work" is all down to a finely tuned balancing act between writers, actors and the director. The core of the drama always revolves around the Lyell Centre's scientific expertise to solve a series of troubling, often violent crimes, usually in the vicinity of London. But why is *Silent Witness* so closely aligned with London? Many believe this was a conscious decision by producers of the series to turn London into a character in its own right, so it can feed into the show's storylines more easily. One veteran TV producer explained: "London is a diverse city full of dramatic potential and it is evolving all the time just like *Silent Witness* itself. I know some people wish it was located in another area of the UK but London is at the heart of everything on the show and it provides a unique canvas. In fact, I'd go so far as to say that if it wasn't located in London then the series itself might have run out of steam by now. It's that important to *Silent Witness*'s success."

THE EPISODE THAT NEVER WAS

In 2012, the most controversial of all episodes was filmed at a cost of almost £2 million. But it was never actually aired. For *Silent Witness* had unintentionally encroached into a real-life crime case that almost plunged the show into the centre of a real-life scandal.

The two-part episode, called "And Then I Fell in Love", was scrapped at the last minute because it too closely mirrored an actual child sex grooming case in Rochdale, in the north of England. This much-anticipated *Silent Witness* two-parter had featured Dr Nikki Alexander stumbling across a sinister underworld where teenage girls were groomed for sex and forced into prostitution. The comparisons to the real case were pretty obvious. The BBC were obliged to replace the two-part special with a repeat because of resemblances between the story and that of the case of nine men accused of a child sex exploitation ring.

BBC bosses decided it would be "too insensitive" to show the episode over the bank holiday weekend of 6 and 7 May 2012, as the trial of the men hadn't yet come to a close at Liverpool Crown Court. The corporation did not want to take any legal risks, as is the way with most factual and non-factual television these days. It was possible that the episodes in question might be seen as influencing the decision of the jury in that trial. This meant the programme could be risking a contempt of court accusation.

After the BBC had slotted two repeat episodes in place of the child grooming shows, a message was even posted on the BBC website stating: "We are aware of enquiries from viewers who want to know when the two-part *Silent Witness* episode 'And Then I Fell In Love' will be shown." But the real reason for the switch was not announced in public and, as a result, many viewers were left angry by the sudden decision to drop a new story they'd been looking forward to seeing. Some viewers even took to social media message boards to vent their frustration at the unexplained absence of this highly anticipated two-parter.

The court case in Liverpool heard how vulnerable girls as young as 13 – including some from care homes – had been given sweets, alcoholic drinks and drugs to lure them into having sex with men who passed them around to other men like objects. The court was told the abuse – which began in 2008 – had taken place at two takeaway restaurants in Rochdale. Some of the girls were beaten and forced to have sex with "several men in a day, several times a week". One teenager told the jury she was forced to have sex with 20 men in one night. Another recalled being raped by two men while she was "so drunk she was vomiting over the side of the bed".

The jury at the Liverpool Crown Court trial eventually returned with guilty verdicts for the nine men, aged between 24 and 59. Their offences included rape and child sex trafficking and exploitation. They were each sentenced to up to 25 years in prison.

As a result of this incident, *Silent Witness*'s producers and writers became even more careful about using any topical material, in order to avoid the problems they faced back in 2012.

The furore about the similarities between the scrapped *Silent Witness* episode and that real-life court case provoked a wider debate about whether *Silent Witness* and other popular forensic TV dramas such as *CSI* influence the judgement of juries in murder trials. One forensic scientist explained: "I think TV dramas may well have made juries become too over-presumptuous, when it comes to multiple forensic evidence on every case. If the forensic evidence doesn't prove someone guilty that seems to be a game changer. Jury members will often find a defendant not guilty if there is no forensic evidence, even when the police have found their own proof that someone is guilty." The same forensic expert added: "It's dangerous to always rely on forensic evidence. This must be connected to what they've seen on programmes like *Silent Witness*, during which forensic evidence is virtually a prerequisite when it comes to achieving a successful prosecution or defence for that matter."

"THE GREATER GOOD" FINALE

In the final episode of *Silent Witness* series 23 – aired just before the Coronavirus pandemic threw the entire world upside down in the spring of 2020 – the show saw one main character die and another quit.

Millions of viewers were completely blindsided by the sudden death of Dr Thomas Chamberlain, played by Richard Lintern, 57, who'd become one of *Silent Witness*'s most popular characters since arriving in the laboratory back in 2014. His end came when he choked to death in front of Nikki Alexander and forensic researcher Clarissa after being exposed to a nerve agent that was contained in a vial lodged in the throat of a dead body. Dr Chamberlain bravely prevented Nikki and Clarissa from entering the lab, so that they did not get poisoned, before he died moments later. One viewer wrote on social media: "That's one of the most harrowing death scenes ever on TV. Didn't even really like Thomas and am completely in bits." Another viewer added: "I've never felt so heartbroken watching *Silent Witness*."

And in the middle of this highly dramatic episode, quirky forensic expert Clarissa Mullery announced she was resigning, which stunned many fans of the series. It was later revealed that actress Liz Carr – who has a rare condition called arthrogryposis multiplex congenita – had decided to leave the show after 10 successful seasons because she'd been offered a major part in a Hollywood sci-fi blockbuster called *Infinite*, alongside Mark Wahlberg and Oscar-winner Chiwetel Ejiofor. Liz's character Clarissa was a highly observant and efficient scientist, whose meticulous eye for detail had helped the Lyell Centre team solve many murders. She was super-organized and full of healthy sarcasm. Her encyclopaedic knowledge of forensic cases and advancements in the field made her a formidable team member. Clarissa's exit resulted in her screen husband Max, played by Daniel Weyman, having to leave the show. Explaining her surprise decision, actress Liz Carr later said: "To quote Clarissa, 'I just know, deep down – that it's time for me to move on, to focus less on the dead and more on the living. On life'."

Viewers were left on tenterhooks at the end of that same episode as to whether Jack – played by David Caves – would survive having been exposed to the same nerve agent that killed Tom. The last shot of him was in a hospital intensive care unit.

* * *

But what does the future hold for *Silent Witness* itself? Actress Emilia Fox's ongoing starring role as pathologist Alexander seems to be set in stone – for the time being. Her character continues trying to cement her transatlantic love affair with

Matt Garcia (played by Michael Landes), whom she met a couple of series back. Meanwhile – despite the interruptions caused by the worldwide Coronavirus outbreak – many are keenly anticipating *Silent Witness*'s next two series, although it looks unlikely the twenty-fourth series will be screened on schedule at the beginning of 2021. This is due to be followed by a twenty-fifth anniversary series in 2022.

ENDLINES

HIGH TECH

TV's *Silent Witness* is renowned for its obsession with the technical side of pathology, and the programme has highlighted much of the latest, genuinely ground-breaking equipment available to forensic investigators.

A team of British and Canadian researchers has recently managed to successfully sequence the full genome of a living organism using a machine the size of a smartphone called the MinION. This "DNA sequencer" fits in the palm of your hand, and is a major breakthrough because it enables more personalized medical diagnosis and better research in the forensic field. The machine is currently undergoing tests to evaluate its efficiency. Its tiny size and relatively low cost could allow scientists to perform much more advanced analysis outside a lab. It can even be attached to a laptop via a USB cable. It is expected that further research work will be required to iron out any teething problems, although it's highly likely this equipment will be openly available by the middle of 2021.

Another important new piece of equipment is a 3D Crime Scene Scanner that sends out a laser that bounces off all surfaces in a room and can be used to accurately recreate a crime scene up to 130 metres away. It's claimed this machine can predict where an item was placed once the crime scene is viewed through the scanner. The scanner can also be used to show a jury in a court case an actual projected crime scene without them having to visit that specific location. This is from the point of view of someone standing in the middle of the actual room where a crime was committed. The 3D Crime Scene Scanner is able to highlight the flight path of blood or bullet projectiles. The trajectory of a bullet is shown in three dimensions. Forensic scientists say this is an enormous leap from a technical standpoint, because real experts and those on *Silent Witness* were using earlier versions of the scanner, but this new model is said to be many more times sophisticated.

RECRUITMENT DRIVE

Many in the world of law and order believe that *Silent Witness* has had a positive effect on improving the UK's crime detection rates, because so many more people are today working inside crime laboratories, which has greatly improved the efficiency of those facilities. There are more applications for jobs in the forensic sector than ever before. I've personally met three people under 30 working in forensic science in recent months, which seems to prove that point.

An assistant inside a laboratory at entry level is usually paid around £15,000 to £20,000 a year. They can eventually end up becoming a Reporting Officer, who would earn in the region of £40,000 a year. Training takes 18 months, and any applicant needs at least a 2:2 in a relevant scientific degree to qualify. Many forensic scientists enter the profession with postgraduate degrees in forensics, too.

But this thirst for jobs in the forensic sector *has* rubbed some scientists up the wrong way. They've told me that forensic science students expect to be allowed to participate in actual autopsies before they're anywhere near being qualified to do so. "I'm afraid I have to blame that on *Silent Witness*.

The series rarely shows any of the early stages of a forensic scientist's training," said one forensic investigator:

> It's a pity because I've encountered so many young people not prepared to put in the hard graft at the boring end of what we do, before they're even allowed a hint of direct involvement in a genuine case. You can't encourage youngsters to hack at corpses until they're properly trained. A lot of these young would-be forensic scientists seem to think they'll be allowed to take part in autopsies within a few weeks of starting training. I always say to them at that stage "welcome to the real world".

DNA DAY

The genetics "industry" is considered so vital to the future of the United States of America that there is now a National DNA Day holiday in April every year to commemorate the completion of the Human Genome Project in 2003 and the discovery of DNA's double helix in 1953.

The Human Genome Project was an international scientific research project that determined the base pairs which make up human DNA. This enabled scientists to identify and map out all of the genes belonging to the human genome from both a physical and practical standpoint.

The double helix is the twisted-ladder structure of DNA. Its discovery in 1953 marked a milestone in the history of science and led to modern molecular biology, which revolved around how genes control the chemical processes within a human body.

The intention of the current public holiday in the United States is to encourage students, teachers, and the public to learn more about genetics and genomics and perhaps even plan for a career in that sector.

THE PERFECT MURDER

After extensively researching and writing this book, it's become clear that the world of forensic science is split down the middle when it comes to one highly emotive question connected to their expertise: *Is it possible to commit the perfect murder and get away with it?*

Law enforcement would have us believe the killers of the world are much less likely to get away with murder than 30 years ago. But is that really true? The fact is that while you've been reading this book, someone, somewhere has committed the perfect murder, for which they will never be arrested. Often, we don't even discover if their victim died at the hands of another human being. They could appear to have died in a road accident or by drowning in the sea or any of dozens of other ways, which could easily disguise the real cause of a death. Yet – you may well ask – surely advances in forensic science and investigation techniques in recent years mean that it's harder to get away with murder?

"We're scientists, not murder squad detectives," one London forensic scientist explained. "And it isn't our job to prevent crimes from being committed. All we can do is highlight the scientific evidence of a crime and hope that our efforts will lead to justice for the victim. I've got no doubt murders will continue to be committed at a fairly steady rate because most of them occur within families where emotions run high. Worrying about forensics is not something those type of killers bother themselves with. These are people who commit their crimes on impulse, without even considering the consequences." One former London murder squad detective explained: "We will never live in a crime-free world. Most murderers only get caught because they confess their crimes to someone else. And in my opinion, most of those killers are asking to be caught anyway."

Back to the whole question of a supposedly perfect murder scenario. Most forensic scientists I spoke to for this book refused to speculate or offer any advice because it went against their ethics. But one expert did have this to say:

It's not so hard, even today, to get away with murder. Obviously, you have to clean every aspect of the crime scene before you leave and there are other things you'd have to remember. But the most important aspect of all is to get rid of the body in such a way it can never be found and that is a lot easier said than done! Just throwing it in a river or burying it is obviously not going to work in the long run. One of the hardest cases I ever had to investigate involved a gang of professional criminals, who employed a specialist 'body remover' after every murder. He used acid to disperse every single part of a body and the

raw liquid that was left was added to regular fertiliser, which was sold legitimately at garden centres.
The brilliant aspect of all this was the way everything
was spread around. It was impossible to track down
where it all ended up and even if we had found a few
bags, then finding actual DNA in them would have
been virtually impossible because it had been effec-
tively 'watered down' by the fertiliser.

The same forensic scientist added: "The only reason I know
all this is because one of the gang members decided to inform
on his associates and he stated all this in court. But none of it
was ever proved because we couldn't find any trace of DNA in
the supposedly relevant fertiliser."

Some other forensic scientists have admitted to me that
they use the challenging question of the perfect murder to help
them during their own investigations. "Sometimes you need
to try and get inside the head of a criminal in order to find out
more about the crime they have committed. It's the ultimate
intellectual challenge if you work in this field of forensics,"
said one US-based pathologist. "I often try to run through
the thought process of the killer on a case. If he believed he
was committing the perfect murder, he would have ticked
off certain boxes, at least in his head. I try to work my way
through what those were. That gives me a clearer picture of
what the killer did at certain stages during his or her crime."

NEVER TO BE
FORGOTTEN

The priority of all forensic scientists is to apply their technology to establish accurate information that reflects the events that occurred at a specific crime scene. Various disciplines of forensic science have made a unique contribution towards investigating a wide range of crimes, but it is worth remembering the genocide and other mass killing offences throughout the world over the past three decades that also relied on the expertise of some of these scientists.

Forensic archaeologists have in recent times visited Rwanda, Argentina, Bosnia, Kosovo and Croatia. Their skills were essential to achieve victim identification. The aim of these specialists was to extract evidence from vast numbers of victims of those atrocities that might help investigators track down those who were responsible for their deaths.

This meant scientists having to deal with some of the most barbaric examples of mass murder ever witnessed in modern times. Graves filled with thousands of corpses, multiple skeletons scattered over rough terrain, the charred remains of innocent children. But they eventually extracted enough secrets from those corpses to help track down the murderous individuals behind these killings and bring them to justice.

These findings were also carefully collated so as to be admissible in a court of law in each country, as well as at the human rights court in The Hague in Holland. As one London forensic scientist said: "Those are the forensic scientists who are really out in the field. They have to sift through vast numbers of human remains looking for evidence of murder. Those are the forensic findings that truly effect history."

FORENSIC HEROES

The Three Musketeers mentioned in the opening of this book and the other characters featured throughout it are not the only forensic pioneers, by any means. Due credit should go to other legendary forensic experts who, down the years, have contributed so much towards the never-ending quest to find out the truth from the dead.

Many of these characters played big roles in developing the world that has enabled *Silent Witness* to exist:

1. DR MATHIEU ORFILA

Dr Mathieu Orfila (1787–1853 – France) developed research work that laid the foundations for toxicology, a vital part of forensic science. His first book *Traité des Poisons*, or *Treatise on Poisons*, propelled the worlds of medicine, chemistry, physiology, and even the legal arena.

2. DR JOSEPH BELL

Dr Joseph Bell (1837–1911 – United Kingdom) would often impress colleagues by using his observation skills to deduce what a patient's occupation was and their recent activities. He was the inspiration for the character of Sherlock Holmes.

3. DR HENRY FAULDS

Dr Henry Faulds (1843–1930 – United Kingdom) published a paper detailing the usefulness of using fingerprints for identification. Dr Faulds later collaborated with Charles Darwin's cousin, Francis Galton, and they established a statistical model of fingerprint analysis.

4. WILLIAM R. MAPLES

William R. Maples (1937–97 – United States) was a forensic examiner specializing in human identification and trauma analysis. He worked on many high-profile cases during the 1800s, including the remains of Joseph Merrick, "The Elephant Man".

5. JOHN GLAISTER

John Glaister (1856–1932 – United Kingdom) applied scientific methods to the examination of trace evidence gathered at crime scenes from the late 1800s into the first quarter of the following century. His work on the identification of hair was a significant breakthrough.

6. FRANCES GLESSNER LEE

Frances Glessner Lee (1878–1962 – United States) is credited with inventing miniature crime scene models in the early 1900s, which homicide investigators used to sharpen crime-solving skills.

7. ROBERT P. SPALDING

Robert P. Spalding (born 1944 – United States) developed bloodstain pattern analysis. In 1971, he joined the FBI, and his contributions changed how crime scenes are investigated.

8. HENRY LEE

Henry Lee (born 1938 – United States) worked on many notorious US murder cases, including the O.J. Simpson investigation. He has a PhD in biochemistry and went to the US specifically to study forensic science.

9. PROFESSOR DAVID BOWEN

Professor David Bowen (1924–2011 – United Kingdom) succeeded musketeer Donald Teare after working as his assistant. Later, he examined human remains that were blocking the drain of a house in Muswell Hill, north London, which led to the arrest of serial killer Dennis Nilsen.

10. SIR WILLIAM WILLCOX

Sir William Willcox (1870–1941 – United Kingdom) was a physician and toxicologist, renowned for his skill with a scalpel and test tube in the first half of the twentieth century. He experimented with patches of human skin, firing different guns at them from different distances to see how this distorted their appearance.

THE AUTHOR

WENSLEY CLARKSON has worked inside the underworld for more than 30 years alongside police officers, forensic scientists and criminals. His research has included prison visits, surveillance operations, police raids and even post-mortems. Clarkson's books – published in more than 30 countries – have sold more than two million copies. He has made numerous documentaries in the UK, US, Australia and Spain, and written TV and movie screenplays. Clarkson's recent book *Sexy Beasts* – about the infamous Hatton Garden heist – was nominated for a Crime Writers' Association Dagger award.

www.wensleyclarkson.com